THE DOUBLE LIFE OF ALFRED BUBER

THE DOUBLE LIFE OF ALFRED BUBER

DAVID SCHMAHMANN

THE PERMANENT PRESS
Sag Harbor, NY 11963

For information, address:
  The Permanent Press
  4170 Noyac Road
  Sag Harbor, NY 11963
  www.thepermanentpress.com

Library of Congress Cataloging-in-Publication Data

Schmahmann, David–
    The double life of Alfred Buber / David Schmahmann.
        p. cm.
    ISBN 978-1-57962-218-3 (hardcover : alk. paper)
        1. Middle-aged men—Fiction. 2. Secrecy—Fiction.
    3. Loneliness—Fiction. 4. Young women—Thailand—
    Bangkok—Fiction. 5. Americans—Thailand—Bangkok—
    Fiction. 6. Man-woman relationships—Fiction. I. Title.

PS3619.C44D68 2011
813'.6—dc22   2011006937

Printed in the United States of America.

For my father and brother,

rare men both

CHAPTER ONE

These are the chronicles of the starship Buber, noted bibliophile, late night television addict, keeper of sordid little secrets so appalling he dares not breathe a word of them to a soul. Gone are the daring thoughts of which there were once an abundance. They once had shape and color and flesh of their own, but time and tiredness have frayed them until all that remains is residue, a creaking membrane of abandoned ideas, a scaffold without substance. Such a careful construct, all in all, destroyed by scandal, scandal that found him unprepared, black-eyed, bloody mouthed, quite flat footed.

Where shall I go, then, if I wish to learn where it is that I went wrong, what I could have done differently? I will say *ab initio*, from the outset, that I have no answer, or none that I can find. My father is long dead, my mother now so alienated that I doubt she would be a resource of any value. And I don't believe in God.

In another room, the next room, Nok sleeps. Or then again, perhaps she does not. Perhaps my bedroom, that chamber of disappointments, is empty. Perhaps there is no one in it, no one at all. In the next room Nok, out of her element, my captive, Buber's little secret, sleeps. One would think, looking down at her smooth little body, her silk hair spread about the pillow, her flimsy linen shirt, that she would meet a raft of needs. But then again, to watch her walk around this great house of the Buber's is, can be, almost comical. She appears to have no interest in anything, no sense of curiosity, to be completely devoid of awe. Her habits too are completely alien, so . . . vulgar. She squats when she reads, and that with difficulty.

And what else should I have expected? A person reaps what he sows, does he not? I have created obscenity in a child scratching for a living, invited shame, and now shame engulfs me. In short, can there be any doubt that I have made a cock-up of things? Even so I am not one to scrounge about in the past for tidbits of memory that might explain it away, mitigate the damage. I mean, one only has to watch television for several minutes to see middle-aged men sniveling about the past as if it had some great, sustaining significance. I do not worship at the altar of psychotherapy, I am afraid to say. I am not, I am afraid, wired for it, even if that is my loss.

The "I" in this, the man at the helm, looks puzzled as a flash of memory intrudes. The memory is this: My mother, happening on me in a state of arousal, begins to giggle. "You don't say," she murmurs. "*Even you.*" Later, at dinner, she ventures to my father: "You and Alfred should have a little chat sometime," and then she begins to giggle again, this time uncontrollably, must leave the room with her hand at her mouth.

Yes, *even me*. Freakish. Extraordinary. Incomprehensible.

Shall I describe my house instead of continuing in this vein? I would prefer to. In fact I would be pleased to. It has been at the center of so much.

When I was a young man—and that means years ago, when I was a struggling immigrant in this austere city—I passed through this town once, down this very lane, and decided that this was where I would one day live. There was something about the place that marked it as my resting place, the place in America I would claim as my own when all else had taken shape. I became quite single-minded, after that, in my planning.

This is something I do not share often, but I slept on a cot in a rooming house for four years to scrape together the money I needed to acquire this fantasy. I spent nothing in those days, did not own a car or a television, or even a telephone, but even so I had no use for flawed hand-me-downs or makeshift possessions and so I surrounded myself with . . . nothing. I was making a fairly good living too, and I know that my father's cousin, Nigel, the only relative I have in this country, thought my behavior, the urgency I felt to buy an empty plot of land in a town with which I had no connection, eccentric, at a minimum. Nigel is, after all, a creature of habit, a rational man, an academic whose view of things is unshakably rooted in good judgment. Each time he asked about my living arrangements in those rooming house days and I gave the kind of oblique answers I did, he would look at me askance and a vaguely troubled expression would cross his face.

"You're a hard-working young man," he used to say, his fork poised at his mouth, his Pritiken grains carefully balanced on the tines. "I imagine a great deal is expected of you at your law firm. How can you look your best when you keep your clothes in a box and be sufficiently rested when you sleep on a stretcher?"

"The arrangements are temporary," I would insist.

"Perhaps," he would say without conceding anything. "They seem immoderate nevertheless."

Once I had bought the land I would come out here from my rooming house by train each weekend. It is a long walk from the station to my little sanctuary, and I would trudge to my destination along the narrow lanes like some Dickensian vagabond.

"May I help you?" the occupant of a rare passing car might stop to ask.

"No thank you," I would say. "I'm all set."

They'd move on, slowly, and I'd see eyes fixed on me in rearview mirrors. Later, as I idled away the time under a tree, I'd see them again, curious, wondering what was

9

afoot, what the stocky bald-headed man in white thought he was doing.

I didn't only daydream, of course, though in the end my efforts were largely undone by bulldozers and backhoes. I moved rocks out of what I knew would someday be a courtyard, tended the sprouts of the elm trees that now line the driveway, used a shovel to level the ground where I planned to place my gazebo. I had yet to lay one brick in place but I had it all staked out, used to stand within the stakes and imagine that my house was already finished, exactly as I had planned it, solid, immovable, like a fortress of marble and glass or a chapel up on a hill. All I thought of then was beauty, the symmetries and contrasts, how the eye would move across a sloping lawn and come to rest on a perfect line of trees.

On several occasions during my Henshaw & Potter days I agreed to host the firm's annual picnic, and believe me I made my impact. I selected the best wines from my cellar, unlocked my most valuable cutlery, placed fresh flowers in every room, and during the course of the day I would steal glimpses at the young clerks as they drifted about the halls, boys clutching the hands of their companions, girls with timid boys in tow, their attention fixed on the art, the sculpture, the views from each towering window.

"Buber," they were doubtless murmuring. "Buber lives *here*?"

They could not have known it, of course, but it was for just such a reaction that they were invited. Buber may have had his deficits, may in some circles have been a subject of derision, but each evening he would retake possession of his museum-like rooms, move about his collection of treasures at will, be in his element.

Surely that counted for something. Surely.

───∞∞∞───

There was from the outset, of course, a woman in this phantom landscape, a singular woman, bonded to me, endlessly understanding, completely intelligent. She was tall and willowy, as I saw her, her face animated, the fabric of her clothing ruffling in the breeze as she leaned back in her chair. I once really did believe that my house would come to hold a family, be a home to children too, the children of this phantom woman and me, be a repository of a host of happy memories. What happened instead, perhaps predictably, was quite different. When all was said and done, when the keys were finally handed over and the last workman had left, there was nobody here to celebrate except me, me in a silk cravat, the bottoms of my trousers rolled, me sipping a congratulatory sherry in a silk-covered chair.

Sometimes I yearn for that other vision, the one I once held for myself, for this house, for everything, with an intensity it would be difficult to describe.

"It was your choice it didn't happen that way," Nigel would say.

"Not entirely," I would have to respond.

As I sat back that first evening and attempted to savor what I had long anticipated as a perfect moment, at that moment, it was early evening, the sky was sheathed in pink, a bird descended and sat on the railing, squawking, littering, its baubles glistening in the light. (*I am rich, you see, in metaphor and allusion. Perverse and secretive men like myself often are even as we dance around what it is we feel we must say, vamping, mocking ourselves, making fun.*) As I saw the young people going respectfully through my rooms I did not need to be reminded that there is sometimes a thin line separating elegance from farce.

⁃⃝⃝⃝⃝⃝⃝⃝⃝

I remember the day I drove my first Mercedes-Benz home from the dealership, the sense of wonder I felt as I watched the little star ahead of me glide through the air. I had dreamed of owning such a machine for a long time and it felt, as I left the lot, that a landmark of sorts had been passed and that the moment signaled, in a most personal way, the end of an epoch.

But as I turned into the traffic something within me spoke up, reminded me that the years immediately past had been complicated but purposive, and that I may yet someday look back on them with more than a modicum of wistfulness.

"Alfie," Nok has said, "I not understand something."

Her accent is quite charming, actually, something breathless in it, something half lost in the consonants.

"What is that?" I ask.

"Everything in house not touch," she responds. "So much things. No one come. Nothing use."

She believes, Nok, that I am endlessly wealthy, and that is no surprise. Everyone does, did so even before and when quite the opposite held true. They have always considered me rich, my new countrymen, picture me I suspect against a backdrop of white-turbaned servants and gold mines and men lounging in wood-paneled rooms. They impose on me a caricature of colonial life, I have always thought, see me as an emissary of the Brittle Empire, have constantly in mind visions derived from English courses and snippets of *Masterpiece Theatre*. I, Buber, a relic of Empire! And to be honest I have, when it has suited me, fed the illusion. When Rhodesia was falling apart and I was asked about it, I would say things that suggested it was my view that an idyllic way of life was indeed coming to an end, that we had something unique in Southern Rhodesia, something unspeakably genteel, something almost perfect in its balance. I adhered, in short, to a vision of a world that did not exist and presented it to others as if it could be reclaimed in an instant.

To my colleagues this flat, fruity, Englishy accent of mine masks a multitude of sins. They think me cultured, steeped in something stronger than I am, and I take it, accept it, and it has made me a stranger. I am hemmed in by the tea and the tweed of it, have sunk into a manner more mannered even than the illusion I myself created. *I have become, in short, a perfect English gentleman.*

12

The irony is rich. I am so much less than I project myself to be, bear no resemblance to the man I have insisted people see me as.

This particular feature of Buber is a closed book to Nok.

How does one say this, put on the table once and for all, and at the outset, that niggling, tedious matter that seems to be an overriding motif of my life? Genetics have decreed, I suppose one could start, that some people will experience their passage on earth one way, and others will experience it another. I have been blessed, one could say, with some measure of ability, some measure of temperament which stands me in good stead in my chosen profession, the law, some measure of financial acumen too. It is all though, I would say, tempered by this: I stand five-foot and six inches high, a portly little chap, balding at twenty, hairless at thirty, my face marked by a nose so large and round and eyes so beady that even at this age, at forty, my reflection startles me. My fingers are short. My legs are hairless. Over the years, the women as they count their money have become more and more businesslike. They count in silence, without smiling. It is a chore, their slouch says, this counting, that other thing, all the same.

(I must temper this image, not the women, the counting, but the other thing, the grotesque little Micawber I have just created of myself. How one sees oneself can be notoriously unreliable, can it not? In the end events must speak for themselves since I may have become too unreliable to add any observation of value. One does not need mirrors, in the end, to know how one believes one looks. I was once called beautiful, as you will see, though that is another matter entirely. I can say this, categorically: The obvious is obvious. I have the full complement of organs, no discernible deformities. I do have about me, as I have said, a certain European melancholy, a spongy civility that is my own invention. For the rest of it, who knows? I stroll over to the mirror to examine once again and it casts back a blank, nothing, a shining plate of nothing.)

13

As a boy in Salisbury, of course, such things were of marginal importance. For one thing I was among my own, or so it seems in retrospect; and even if it were true that my defect had already manifested in some form, it did not seem to foreshadow the future if the little girls teased others coyly and let me be. I was the class clown, or at least the teachers characterized it as such, and that brought a measure of popularity, a certain notoriety as we moved through the senior grades; but it is simply a fact that I do not know the feeling of being looked at admiringly by the opposite sex. Those who take such things for granted cannot appreciate how one might react once one has come to terms with this. One no longer dresses with an eye to winning admiration but rather works to create an alternative image, whether this be well-tailored, impeccably groomed, or something quite other. In my case it is to be self-contained. What I mean by this is that I pack myself into my clothing so as to appear to be wholly complete, to lack nothing, to be beyond need. Such an edifice is flawed. Of course it is flawed.

I approach women warily, regard them as somewhat adverse to me in interest, on the verge of mockery.

———

I omit one thing. Once, it is true, just once, there was someone who seemed genuinely drawn to me. When I was in primary school in Salisbury a new girl joined the class, a stranger looking creature than we had ever seen to be perfectly honest, the product of a Rhodesian mother and a Japanese father. I don't know how her parents came to be together, what the circumstances of it were, but either way one day dark, muscular Rosalind showed up and was given the desk next to mine. I wonder if the boys with whom I went to school, none of whom, so I understand, remain in Rhodesia, would own up to it, but I distinctly remember words such as half-caste and mongrel being bandied about behind the cricket field scoreboard. The girls too, as I recall it, avoided Rosalind when first she came.

I picture her as she stood beside her desk on that first day, her matte brown hair, her dusky skin, her clay-colored eyes. I remember her teeth, her lips, her thick braid. We may have been twelve. Because she was given the desk next to mine the teachers assumed that I would be of assistance in acclimating her, and I was. I remember her handwriting, painstakingly neat, the scent of her, of her hair as I leaned over to show her how to complete an assignment. I was a popular enough boy then, I would remind you, still completely at ease among my own.

"Ask your girlfriend if her thing goes sideways too, Alfie," I remember being teased.

My girlfriend, what a concept, and in a way over time she became, if not that, something not far removed from that. I remember thinking it worth the taunts to play marbles with her on the edge of the playing field, appreciated how she would crouch, a knee peeping from under her dark green uniform, to shoot at the targets we set ourselves. I remember feeling the warmth of her as we stood beside our respective desks each sun-filled morning to greet the teacher. I remember how the sun would hit the top of her head and turn her hair almost gold, make it almost translucent.

I was aware of her, in short, keenly, and began to sense that she was aware of me too. Oh, it was school-boyish enough, to be sure. She would bring things for me from home, a piece of cake or a new notebook, and I would carry her suitcase to the bus, sense the brush of her as she took back the handle from my hand. I was of an age to notice the other things too, features of hers that later in my life in other women were to become such a constant intrusion, the faint lines of underwear beneath a cotton blouse, the almost unbearably delicate fingers, the curve of the muscle above the knee as it touched the hem of her skirt. But these were not the things that won my heart, plunged me into something approaching love. It was her sweetness, rather, her solicitude, her concern that she might be holding me up or inconveniencing me, her gratitude.

"I don't know why you're being so kind to me," she said one afternoon as I tried to explain something we had learned before she arrived. "I'm just thick, is all. I never get things."

"That's not true," I insisted there in that empty classroom, she beside me at the desk, the sounds of an African man polishing the floor coming from the corridor outside. "I think you're cleverer than most."

"You think so, really?" she had said and turned to me, her face now almost unbearably large, her eyes shining inches from mine.

Her knee grazed against mine as she turned and my heart, if it were not contained, would have leaped away.

"Of course," I said, and my voice lost its timbre, was scarcely a whisper, and then there was a moment of quiet, of perfect quiet in which anything was possible, anything at all, and then the door opened and the cleaning man came in with his big machine and began to polish the floor.

The moment did not repeat itself and instead, as I replay all this, summer arrived just then and with it the athletic season, never my strong suit. In a place where physical prowess, sports, were paramount, Rosalind showed herself to be almost indefatigable, to have stamina quite unlike anything they had seen at the school before. She ran at a brisk and steady clip, her muscular little legs a whir as she took off around the track; and as the other girls tired and slowed she would keep at it, complete a cycle, set out on another, keeping an easy steadfast beat. People would drift over to watch, mouths would tighten, admiring things would be said. Even if her parents had not left Salisbury quite unexpectedly before the term was over, I began to suspect that she may be moving irretrievably beyond my grasp. I remember wondering, sitting there on the stands and witnessing it all, what she was thinking—the tiny figure whirling along on the far side of the track—what filled her thoughts as she spun along so increasingly out of reach. I knew what had begun to fill mine.

It was common knowledge that her family's return to Salisbury was not a success. You see, it was her father who was Japanese while her mother was Rhodesian and now, all these years later, I have come almost to believe that had it

16

been the other way round, had her father been Rhodesian and her mother Japanese, the family's reception in Salisbury might have been warmer. Either way even my perennially isolated parents knew something of it, how her father, an engineer, could not find work, and of her mother's deep unhappiness.

She told me first, Rosalind, before she told anyone else, that they were leaving, going to England.

"We can write," she had said, "and one day you'll visit."

I agreed, attempted to act with appropriate nonchalance, felt the unexpected heat of her lips on my cheek as she leaned over, unexpectedly, impulsively, to kiss me goodbye. I will not soon forget the sight of her, the silhouette of her head as she sat buckled into the back of her parents' white Volkswagen and shrank away to nothing down the muddy street.

All so long ago, so dated, so stale, so mildewed. Come then, sit by Ebenezer Scrooge and me among the spirits of the might-have-beens.

"That style's a little dated," a tailor might say of my Ebenezer Scrooge suit, perfect cashmere, impeccably cut. "Is sir certain he won't try something a little more contemporary?"

Sir looks at himself in the mirror. Yes, sir is certain.

I have been asked on several occasions to run for the town's Board of Aldermen. There were reasons I would not have done it even if I had been inclined to. How deep would one's opponent dig to find the information that would damage one? I was always careful, but even master criminals slip up. How much more so the short, round, oro-tund, Alfie Buber?

That is all moot now.

Did I just hear Nok stir in another part of the house?

—⚬⚬⚬—

This is an honest chronicle. It would be pointless if it were not, on that we are agreed. Captain James T. Kirk,

17

whom I watch on occasion at three in the morning, is scrupulous in the accuracy of his log, and so too will I be.

This squat pillar of the church is a whoremonger—and more too. An expert, an exploiter, a skirt chaser, almost certainly a pederast though not by design, an addict. I have come to see life as a series of exchanges only, a long list of trade-offs so that sex for money is just a corner of it and nothing remarkable at all. Is it any wonder, then, that things should have ended the way they have, in a kind of disgrace that seems to have been tailor-made for me?

Oy.

Let me start at the beginning, though of course there is no certain beginning. You will forgive me, I hope, at the outset at least, my one glaring omission: *You.* One does not need, does one, to tell the Mona Lisa that she hangs on a wall? But I will be complete because, you see, my dearest, if you are reading this it is because you are here after an absence of a lifetime during which I scarcely knew, did not know, that you existed; and I am gone, beyond reproach and blame, beyond sin and virtue, beyond the reach of judgment good and bad. I did not set out, I will say here and now, to place this before you, specifically. Much of it is not appropriate, I am well aware, for your eyes. But everything is now yours and eventually you will find these notebooks. You may read them. You may not. Maybe you will place them on a heap somewhere, in a plastic bag in the alley waiting for disposal.

What does it matter? If you are reading, if you are not reading, I am moldering.

If you have opened these notebooks, *Buber lign in drerd.* And good on it too.

In fact, let's do it this way.

I was born, as I have already intimated, in Africa, in a place known as Rhodesia, now Zimbabwe. I was thirteen when the colonists declared the country independent of Britain, an action my parents stridently opposed though I should admit fairly frankly that they were Communists and therefore often disaffected as a matter of habit. But a smoldering guerilla war of several years duration did follow, and when my call-up papers from the Rhodesian army arrived, the discussion was not whether I would serve but to which country I would go.

"Why not England?" I remember asking.

Several of the boys in my school were English. My parents knew nothing of Rosalind, of course, but England had for me its own furtive charms.

"He could stay with my sister," my mother suggested.

"England?" my father snorted. "You suggest England? In spite of what the English have done to this continent? How Harold Wilson lies to the world, deceives, pretends to oppose what has happened here while making sure he does nothing that might upset it?"

"Alfred says he might like to go to university there," my mother said, always tentative, always easily bullied. "He doesn't have to take prime minister Wilson's side."

My mother often spoke about me in the third person. She tended to treat me as a visitor in the house, someone who had changed her routine, uncomfortably but fortunately not permanently. "Alfred was sent to the principal's office for misbehaving," she might say to my father. "Perhaps he would like to tell you about it."

I remember wondering, as they debated my future, whether to weigh in with my own arguments, but I did not. My preferences never made much difference where my father was concerned.

"The English and their class-driven institutions are corrupt to the core," he insisted. "He's not going to England," and so I came here, to America, but as some sort of spectator, not as an immigrant.

My father's last words at the rickety airport in Salisbury made this clear.

"America is a foul country," he said of a place he had never visited, as the little plane that would carry me to Johannesburg and my flight to New York whirred on the tarmac. "Take it all in if you wish, but don't be seduced by it. There's work to be done here."

He gave no thought to the possibility that black Rhodesians might have no need for someone like me if ever they happened to be free, or indeed to the possibility that I might, over time, come to disagree with his view of things. He seemed, as well, to pay no mind to the irony of it all, that as he pontificated he was, in the end, just a Jew from Europe, allowed into Rhodesia on sufferance. I found out soon enough as well that what he knew of America was the stuff of caricature.

Perhaps he suspected we would not meet again, that day in the airport.

"Have a little fun too," he managed to sputter, his emotions threatening to get the better of him as I started out across the apron. "It won't kill you."

He was, after all, almost sixty, a chain-smoking, florid man with passionate convictions and a menial job. Money for international travel was not something we had in my family in those days.

One didn't need much in the way of documentation to get by in Salisbury when I was a boy; and I suppose that in my father's view of things, in his disdain for authority, such matters as visas were trifles. Something tells me that after all this time I should be able to chuckle at the memory of this, at a stubbornness that in the end resembled naïveté more closely than it did anything else. But there would be more than a touch of bitterness to any humor I might attempt. I was just seventeen, after all, and a very long way from home.

"Where is your visa?" an official at Kennedy airport demanded as she paged through my passport.

"Whatever I have is in there," I said.

"How'd they let you on the plane, boy?" she asked incredulously.

20

When I travel nowadays I am thick with credit cards, travelers' checks, visa forms. I accumulate these driven by a recollection of that frigid winter's evening. I was kept in a weary office for hours as men in dark uniforms debated my status, listened as they muttered about flights back to Johannesburg, hostels, different kinds of quarantine. Eventually I was released to Nigel's custody, but I was even more disoriented than I might otherwise have been. I was also humiliated and unforgiving.

It was not an auspicious start.

———— ∞ ————

After I had been in his home for a week or two, it became obvious that Nigel was feeling a certain impatience with my situation. He and his wife were childless and lived in a small house not far from the university where he taught, and it was clear that my presence had quickly become an imposition. They had their routines, he and his wife. The neighbors could set their clocks by their brisk afternoon walks, and their quiet drink before dinner had a ritualistic air to it. Simply stated, my presence in their house ruined it all. Nigel had assumed when he was cabled and asked to meet me that I had plans, some idea where I was going, what I would be doing once he had provided temporary shelter; but my father had made no such arrangements. I was simply plopped in Nigel's lap, a problem he had not asked for and one he had no responsibility to resolve.

When he began to understand the dimensions of the problem I posed for him, he became quite concerned.

"Your father seems not to have appreciated that America is a very complex country," he said one night after dinner.

His wife was standing at the sink with her back to us washing the dishes. I knew how carefully she was listening.

"I'm afraid so," I must have replied.

I believe this was after I learned that I could not work without a social security number, that I could not get a social security number until my visa status was resolved, and that

I could not simply enroll at the university as one might have done in Salisbury.

"There are a number of universities in this country," Nigel explained patiently, "of a variety of sizes and disciplines. And all of them are very costly."

I remember how he then apologized for doing so and began to question me quite closely about my plans and expectations, such questions as how much money I had brought with me and what arrangements had been made should I incur medical expenses. As I answered, he ran his hands through his hair and looked as angry as I have ever seen him.

"How could your father have done this?" he began, but then his wife, pausing at the sink, said without turning round, "It's clearly not of his doing. Don't take it out on him."

There were, I discovered, tests to be taken, forms to be completed, lines to be waited in. Nigel, probably because he saw he had no choice, took matters in hand, guided me through the process, eventually succeeded in having me admitted, on scholarship, to a local university.

I never did tell my father what he had done, how badly he had miscalculated.

⁂

The political impasse between Rhodesia and Great Britain had not resolved itself by the time I completed university and so, without giving it much thought, I went on to law school.

"Why law school?' Nigel asked.

"It seems as good a grounding as any," I answered.

Things with Nigel had healed a good deal by then. He did not lose an opportunity to remind me of my beginnings, but I suppose I can say without taking undue credit for it that I applied myself to my studies, did not again roil his household. There were money issues of course, and he was generous within his means. The best I could do in return was to complete all I set out to do as competently as I could.

"Grounding in what?" he had asked, sharing as he did just a touch of my father's antagonism to capital and power.

"I think one only knows that once one has it," I told him, and he had responded: "You're very glib, my friend. But not everything can be reduced to a *bon mot.*"

I would have to say that I had no expectation that I would ever practice law, and that may explain why I enjoyed law school so little. Almost from the outset I found myself isolated from my peers, as they panicked in their little collectives and then relentlessly pursued career options I was convinced had no relevance for me. I came to feel as if I were older than they were, from a different generation almost, and as if what kept me apart was not so much my lack of interest in what they were doing as my increasingly fastidious ways, my escalating reticence. With the exception of one sorry little episode which I shall disinter in a moment — its relevance is obvious, most particularly to you — I would have to say that it was in law school that the die was cast. It was then that I first became aware of how people seemed to consider my colonial roots to be quaint, and the quaintness in my response, the overly prudent, mannered, often squeamish *persona* I seem to have adopted, became a shield behind which I stood as I took in my surroundings. I think I may have been respected rather than liked, relied on rather than included.

One must understand that Salisbury was a sedate little town. It had one main road, one major hotel, a level of civility, an absence of competition that escapes most places nowadays. I tend to see myself against such a backdrop, to measure much of what goes on around me by the rather simple yardsticks of that empire setting.

Only I knew that as my father moved from job to job, sold insurance, then real estate, then savings bonds, my mother hired Matabele women to make beadwork and then carried it from store to store trying to sell it for several shillings apiece.

———

My father died in my final year of law school. No one had told me he was ill and I learned only inadvertently that he had spent his final months wracked by cancer. Not long afterwards my mother packed up her things and returned to England.

"There's not much left for me here," she wrote. "Rhodesia became your father's country and I suppose it still is yours if you desire it. But it was never mine, and certainly there is nothing here to keep me."

After she left, even more so after the country finally won its independence, changed its name, toppled the statues that for me were a part of its landscape, the prospect that I might somehow go back, even for a visit, became remote. And so I became an American, but by accident, so to speak, and not at heart. I live here, but except for my sparkling hermitage I do not feel that I am at home here. I am merely observing, continuing my vigil, waiting for something ineffable.

Perhaps it is that, as much as anything else, that has permitted me, and against every instinct, to defile my surroundings.

⸻

I spend hours preparing my house for Nok's arrival, all the while wondering why, what difference it could make, how she can even evaluate what it is she will see. How, indeed, does one size up a glowing white mansion with elaborate mansards and doors of leaded glass, with granite finishes and handcrafted moldings, when one's frame of reference — and I have seen her frame of reference — is a room the size of a closet with one corner reserved for a hole in the ground and water in a waist-high concrete basin.

I stare out the night window and see myself at the airport, against the wall, lurking in an isolated hallway. I am midwife to the birth into daylight of the worst of my nightmares. The television screen will say she has landed and I will picture her in an airplane aisle somewhere, the subject of speculation, doubtless, some admiration certainly, as the craft empties, as people follow each other down the cold corridors to the customs hall. Even as I sit in my own safe chair and gaze into my pitch-black garden I shudder in horror, suppress an urge to flee. I suppress myself, indeed, function almost without awareness.

She emerges and she is so much smaller than the people around her. She is wearing blue jeans and a cotton shirt, carries a backpack over her shoulders. Her hair is tied about itself in a knot on the top of her head. She is lost, out of context. Her walk, I notice as she crosses the floor, is as much a shuffle as a step. She is wearing high heels with her jeans, clunky Minnie Mouse shoes too large for her presence. The bottoms of her jeans, where they overlap her heels, are frayed.

"Nok," I say softly, gingerly, and hand her the flowers I have brought.

To my astonishment she breaks into a broad smile, a genuine smile of delight, and crosses the floor between us in a series of hurried clicks. We embrace, the straps of her backpack abrading my neck, and she presses her face into my chest.

"I so happy see you," she says. "I think maybe you change mind."

Now why, after all the trouble with the embassy, the paperwork, the long, complex instructions, would I do that? Well, if the truth be told, there have been moments when I wished I could put a hold on the process, but that is different.

"I happy see you too," I say.

She is hugging still and then she does something that brings home starkly, oh so starkly, what it is I have done. There on the floor of terminal E, in my embrace, she reaches around and grabs my bottom through my trousers, moves her hand in a wholly unseemly way. I reach back and take her wrist.

"Not here," I say stiffly. "One does not do such things here."

In Boston there are no open secrets as there are there, only dirty cabs waiting in a line outside, crisp winter air, airport police in heavy jackets blowing whistles and answering questions in terse voices. I see her shudder as we leave the hall, as a biting wind scrapes across her face and leaves on it a look of fear and apprehension. I have not brought, should have thought to bring, something warm to wrap about her. It is cold out there. I will give her my coat.

Is this possible? Can this be possible? As I reach for her, expecting a real person, all I feel is air, nothing but air, clasp my arms around myself and nothing more. What kind of love could this be anyhow, a love of this brown-skinned apparition, this slip of a thing clip-clopping across the floor? How could it be? I know nothing of her. No, not nothing: I know the house on stilts, the toothless father, the grease-stained teak platform with its bed rolls and steaming pits, its vistas of buffalos and frondy trees. But of what truly drives her beyond the most base instincts (the look on her face when she experiences, against all of her will, sexual pleasure, for instance), I know nothing. I know snatches of things of no import. I know that she is almost totally silent in the morning, or is with me, that she yields to my desires with something akin to resignation, or more charitably a judgmentless desire to please, that she responds when I pull her towards me by shifting her weight and obliging, rather like swinging open one of those powered doors that are triggered for the handicapped to open at a touch. Touch it and it swings open.

So it is with Nok, and with similar inanimation. She sits quietly beside me in the car as we drive from the airport, the narrative all internal, all mine, as we sweep along a highway that must appear more or less familiar to her — a motorway is, after all, a motorway — and then turn off onto smaller streets, under canopies of trees and past houses each of which must appear to her to be the size of a hotel. She may take it in or she may not. She says nothing. It is as if she is in a waiting room rather than in a car. Yes the customs officers were respectful though they asked a lot of awkward questions. Yes the bank forwarded the drafts. Yes the tickets were waiting for her. No, she couldn't find warm clothes, not there, hardly even a sweater.

"Are you tired?' I ask, aware that for her day has flipped into night, that she has been on an airplane not only for the first time in her life but for almost twenty-four hours.

"I sleep," is all she says even as I am dying to ask her, "Well. What do you think? How does it look?"

"I told you," I say, "that I live in a quiet place. A very quiet place."

She says nothing, seems as interested in what is in her little plastic purse as in what passes outside.

"I think you will like it here," I add and she turns to me, smiles, says in a tone that is simultaneously grateful and insincere, "I like."

I have played this through in my mind too many times to be at such a loss. I know the stakes, have sifted through them again and again, even in my sleep, and yet oddly her very passivity, her seeming lack of interest in anything, raises them even higher. In her own way, over there, powerless though she may have been in every conventional sense, she was at least mistress of the idiom, aware of the currency in her smile, her body, her faked coyness. It has all evaporated in an airplane ride, though how can one not notice that the skin is still as smooth as powder, the hair as dark against her neck as palm fronds against the sky.

(The raucousness, I want to say, is behind you now, the scratching, the unspeakable debasement. You are safe and therefore you can let go of the things that have made you, at least in my experience, overly mercenary, excessively wary, occasionally coarse. I, Henry Higgins Buber, have this planned down to the last detail. I have laced your drawers with potpourri.)

She crosses her legs at the ankle, looks out the window, back at Buber.

"You very rich man," she says smugly as we turn into my driveway and the Moorish arches come into view, the maroon awnings, the little fountain. "I think that before, but now I see."

I open the door and we step into my foyer with its small Henry Moore and art nouveau chairs. I watch her as she takes it in, Cinderella entering the prince's castle, a blotchy, corpulent prince perhaps, but one of unending chivalry, politeness, generosity. She makes no comment, follows me silently up the stairs to our bedroom.

I lay her battered suitcase on an ottoman, invite her to unpack.

"This is where you can hang your clothes," I say. "Here is a bathroom, just for you."

She looks in through the door, sees the recessed tub, the shrubs that hang above it, the enclosed courtyard with its Japanese stonework and single sculpture.

"Bathroom very clean," she remarks as she surveys a room coated with white marble, a tub crafted from a single block of stone, an expanse of shining floor, a wall of glass.

"Very clean. Clean and big."

I experience a form of vertigo as she says it, as if I am observing something from an uncertain height. It is the only comment she has made, will make, about my house that evening. She takes her suitcase with its decal of Mickey Mouse, broken strap, rusted lock, and lays her things, slowly and with great hesitation, on the counter.

(*A fox darts across my garden, breaks my concentration, disappears into the woods that stand at the edge of the pond below.*)

Later, after some fumbling, some awkwardness, I find myself curled on the far edge of the bed while Nok sprawls diagonally across the mattress. I watch her as she snores lightly, notice blemishes on her skin that I have not seen before, rise carefully and stand over her. I walk to the bathroom, examine my face in the mirror. I see something new, something Dorian Gray-like, a curled lip beneath the giant nose, eyes so dark and deeply sunken they shine with a new malevolence. I return to the bedroom and notice that the sun is rising. It does not seem as if a full night has passed. I have taken the day off from work, and will stay here with her until we both have our bearings. We will walk in the garden, Nok and I, attempt to talk, attempt to find a new understanding, to come to terms with the bargain we seem to have struck. We will walk the lawns, stand by the pond.

I will touch her if the mood is right. We will stay within the gates.

She follows me about, eats, looks at the things I point out to her. After lunch we take a nap. I have excused the housekeeper for a few days and prepare something for us to eat.

"Where are the people?" she asks as the day draws on.

"What people?" I say.

"Other people?" she says. "Only you here."

There is another question that has obviously been percolating, all afternoon if not longer. She weighs asking it, backs off, finally asks. Is it not inevitable that she would? She must learn English, that much is clear.

"Why," she finally plucks up the courage to ask, a trace of wistfulness in her voice, "you not marry? You so rich."

She looks unspeakably bashful as she asks it, possibly afraid I might think she has the temerity to be suggesting that this is an aspiration she might possibly harbor herself.

(*I see the face of Arthur Henshaw, the senior partner in my firm, picture Nigel listening as I try to explain to a young girl raised in a shack on stilts why she cannot hope to live as the wife of Henshaw's partner, as the new niece of Nigel the Terrible.*)

I hesitate, cannot find words of appropriate obliqueness to respond. I suppose, in retrospect, that I am as unforthcoming as she is in revealing those things I have come to take for granted. How could I tell her, for crying out aloud, why I am not married or more to the point, why she is here, what she is doing here, what is expected of her? Sexual accommodation, after all, and especially for her, is a commodity of such banality, such constant triviality, that it would never, could never, drive a decision of magnitude. It certainly cannot explain her presence in Boston, even as it may go some of the way to explaining my presence in her city. I know as well that there is a gulf between fascination and love, between loneliness and love, between resignation and love, and that with a woman such as this lust lurks to cloud everything. But can it be love when the path to this moment has been so jagged, from leathered rooms to the menageries in the forest, from oh so proper propriety to scenes so surreal, so incongruous, that they require screeds of context simply to shelter them from appearing ridiculous?

Can it?

It is money, of course, that has brought us to this point, earnest law firm income hard earned by the hour. Money is of course fungible, but who would have dreamed, who ever would have dreamed, that Buber would put it to such a use? And yet she is here. Let us play it out as it goes.

"Buber brought a whore back from Asia? Are you mad?"

"It's true. I have unassailable proof."

"But he's never even been to Asia. He goes to Paris all the time. Doesn't he have a place there?"

"That's what he says. *I* don't think he's ever set foot in France."

"Buber went whoring in Asia. Whoever would have guessed it? Shall we spray his office with Lysol?"

Chapter Two

As I intimated I have omitted something, though the events at issue have not been, not for years, far from my thoughts. They manifest from time to time as insects, little birds, things that hover and flitter and fail to coalesce.

We need to return to the law school for this, an awful little place high on a hill in the middle of nowhere.

I did not attend, as I have said, with any measure of enthusiasm. I applied, was admitted, when the time came drove the rusty Beetle I owned in those days through New York State and arrived just in time for classes. I went to learn a trade, simply put, to maintain my visa status, more than anything else to wait, I do not know for what.

I watched those around me, several years younger than I was for the most part, as they tackled the various trumped-up little conundrums we had to solve, as they pondered the hypothetical questions and argued and analyzed into the night. Perhaps it is true that the rigid and unimaginative education I had received in Salisbury was what the masters said it would be, because it all came easily to me, uninterested as I was, did not seem to justify the scurrying and the worry. I attended classes, returned to my room, read what had been assigned, and in the end I think I was noticed for the first time only when grades were announced. The quiet, sallow man off to the side had surprised.

But that is not the point of this digression. Foreigners on American campuses were quite rare in those days; as I recall I was one of only three or four. Veronica was one of the others. For obvious reasons I now describe her with apprehension, but I did not like her at all on first impression, to be candid, not much more later either as I think on it. She seemed petulant, narcissistic in a uniquely childlike way with her pouting face and small, mincing steps, so that those behind her had always to wait as she made her way, as if meandering down a path, between the desks in the auditorium. She was very small too, like a doll indeed, and one had to strain to hear her when she spoke. She came, or so I learned, from Hong Kong and her English was impeccable though slightly accented in that strange Hong Kong manner with its English-sounding vowels and Chinese glossing over of consonants. ("My father have a Rolls Roy," she once told me.) She wore elaborate clothes, knitted caps, buckled shoes, socks to her knees, but I must say that her hair was quite striking, a black curtain down her back. She had pinned in it, invariably, a flower of sorts.

We first spoke in a waiting room outside an office where one went to have some form or other stamped. She held out her hand, a small limp thing, a pale arm, and introduced herself.

She was also, need I say this, as an Asian woman, an object of immense attraction to me.

———

How does one get from that moment to the other in her bedroom with us both, startled by what we are doing, half undressed?

Forgive me, please.

If I say that she was tone deaf in class, that she consistently raised her hand to answer questions that were meant to be rhetorical, that she came to be regarded with bemusement by the men and to be disregarded by the women, I do not say this to be gratuitously unkind. I was, after all, an oddity myself, but hers was a striking, regressive, Kewpie presence, wrapped as it was in silk and flowers, with bright trinkets and notebooks covered in fabric, assignments decorated with reds and golds, a fish out of water. I gravitated to her for reasons that may be suspect, and if it was because I felt protective in the end, it was obviously me from whom she needed protection. *(Come sit on my knee, little waif, and tell me of your hardships while I touch you.)*

Perhaps I will skip to something that occurred after our transgression, something that alarmed me and made me most deeply regret my actions. She telephoned one afternoon and asked me to come to her apartment because she had something to show me; and when I walked into the room it had been decorated with cards, dozens of heart-shaped cards, one of which was signed "Prince Charles."

"I know him, you know," she said. "When he was in Hong Kong I was his official consort."

"My dear girl," I wanted to say, "the royal entourage does not look to the daughter of a local paper cone magnate to provide consortium for a Prince of Wales."

Of course I said nothing. One cannot dispute that sort of thing, does not expect to be called on to do so, but I knew — anyone would know — that this plain and childlike girl could have been no such thing, would not be receiving a Hallmark card with a simple signature in this manner. Poor thing was, in short, as deluded as I was.

I may have — I did — keep my distance after that, but several days later she called again to say that she had cut her hand seriously and might indeed lose it. I was not permitted to visit or to see her, but a week later, under copious layers of bandage, she did gingerly display a palm lined with Mercurochromed creases and relayed a story about plastic surgery on skin that could not possibly have healed so completely, red markings aside, in so short a period of time.

—❦—

I cannot say whether she was dissembling that afternoon or whether this was simply part of her presentation—ask her if you care to—but after a criminal law class in which rape had been discussed, she asked me several questions that made it clear she had no idea what fornication consisted of.

"How is this possible?" I remember saying. "Didn't your parents discuss it with you? Didn't the other girls in your high school talk about such things? Didn't it ever come up while you were at university?"

She looked at me in that wide-eyed way, pursed her lips like a child sucking candy, shrugged.

"No," she said and then, lapsing into some sort of Chinese pidgin that she may have thought endearing, sucking in her cheeks, asked: "How you find out?"

I cannot recall—I do not wish to recall—what followed. There was a discussion on the sofa in the little apartment she rented above a store on the main street, a discussion that seemed to provoke astonishment, disbelief, that advanced, deteriorated one might say, into a series of whispered, awe-struck exchanges riddled with possibility, and a prickly, guilty, pleasurable sense of absolute prohibition. I noticed then, of all times, the line in her shirt as she reached up, the varied tightnesses in the fabric of her trousers as she sat cross-legged on the sofa, the fragrance and texture of her hair. Do I mitigate or worsen things by adding that at the time I wondered, sat there wondering, whether what I was witnessing had to do with her foreignness itself, so naive was I, wondering whether there may not be indeed, accompanying the strange and immature affect, equally strange and unpredictable appetites and practices. I imagine also, candidly now as an almost-old man, that the thrill in it may have been akin to the addictive rush of the pederast and the pervert. I preyed on her, in short, though I would quickly add that what occurred was more a spilling than a culmination, something inadvertent, embarrassing, not joyful, not satisfying, merely clumsy, oh so awkward, so sticky, so awful.

Thereafter, riven with remorse, I stayed away, away that is until I was called back to view the messages from Prince Charles, the injury to the hand. You may then also understand the sense of horror I felt when she reported, not long afterwards, black-eyed and sobbing, that she was pregnant. In light of Prince Charles, the non-surgery, I did not believe it, but I was panicked nevertheless and my panic abated only slightly when she added that she was leaving immediately for Hong Kong and that she would not return.

I was given to understand that an abortion had been arranged. I did not know what to believe. When she implied that there was something deliberate on my part in what had happened, said in her coy and implacable voice that there was nothing I could do, ever, to set things right, I let it go.

I am ashamed of this, but it happened. I dreamed last night that I was back in law school, in one of those auditoriums with semi-circular rows of seats; the room, in fact, in which I had studied contracts, except that the people in the rows of seats about me were not the law students I studied with, but people I have met since then, my law partners, people whose season ticketed seats surround mine at the symphony, others. I'm not sure what was being discussed, something serious and interesting, and then Veronica beside me lifts her hand to be heard and begins to talk, and whatever it is she says I find it so strikingly banal and disconnected that I cover my ears, try not to hear it, become deeply ashamed as if somehow I were responsible for the content, somehow responsible for all of it.

You know, of course, that this was not the end of it.

CHAPTER THREE

I worked long and hard in those early rooming house days, left at the same time each morning, rarely returned before nine or ten at night. My view of the future had changed, I must say, from a sense that everything around me was temporary, not terribly important, to the realization that I had nowhere else to go, nowhere else I wanted to go. Indeed, I used to have nightmares in those early days of Arthur Henshaw walking into my office and telling me, firmly and without emotion, that I should clear my desk and leave the building; and I could feel myself, though fast asleep, standing on the sidewalk, briefcase in hand, with nowhere to turn but to Nigel, back to the little bed in his basement where I had started out. Perhaps this fragility has to do with memories of my mother and her little boxes of beads, of my father sorting his bills at the dinner table. But it was a nightmare I doubt was shared by the other young lawyers whom I used to watch going off together for drinks or to baseball games at the Fenway stadium.

Very early on, for whatever reason, Arthur Henshaw took me under his wing. (Years later, when I had assumed, if only briefly, his seat at the head of the partners' table, I came across a note he had made the day I came into the office for an interview. "Hire Now!!!" he had written across the top of my evaluation.) I would have to admit that regardless of how courtly and kind he was, I found it awkward when he and I were alone in a room. I found his casual questions, about my weekend, my interests, Rhodesia, difficult. There was something about him that unnerved me, embarrassed me, but I tried to overcome it, made conversation, drank in his praise as if it were all that mattered.

"Have a pleasant evening, Alfred," he might say as he passed my office at the end of the day, wearing his overcoat, a hat, carrying an umbrella.

"I will sir, and you too," I would respond and I could tell, though he had passed out of my line of vision, that he was smiling, happy to be called 'sir,' and by me, satisfied with his protégé.

Sometimes he would stop for a moment before he passed on.

"Interesting plans for the weekend?" he might ask, and I would smile, nod, provide an answer of some vague sort or other. I knew that *he* had plans, Arthur Henshaw, that dressed in his plaid pants and colorful sweaters he would be taking off in his sailboat to cruise across the harbor, his wife at his side, his daughter and her friends atop deck, all of them drinking from tall glasses and watching the seagulls as they trailed the mast.

"Well, see you Monday," he would say, and that would be it.

As I prepared to leave, tidied my desk, put on my waist-coat and jacket, a sense of foreboding would descend. You have to understand how rough is the transition from an office in which you are "Yes Mr. Bubered" and "No Mr. Bubered" up and down by polite young secretaries to another world, one in which you would not warrant a second glance from those same young women. I might be showing a client to the elevator (so courtly: "Please do call if you have questions, at any time. I would welcome it.") and happen to catch sight of a secretary's calf, dwell on it for a wistful moment too long, be slapped away by a querulous look or some random question. I coveted them, how could I not, the ones who worked the machines and took my dictation, the young women fresh from law school who hung on my every word as if it were profound; but I acted as if (how do I explain this? The times demanded it) I were impervious to such things, to the gentle voices and the perfumes, the short skirts and the dipping blouses, the eyes, the hair, the graceful smiles.

The building is serviced each evening by a small army of Spanish-speaking women ('Sandinistas,' the young lawyers call them), who trundle their carts down the hall, swap out plastic liners, flap dusters about bookshelves.

A girl enters to clean my office. This is a new girl, young, delicate, very fair. As she moves about the room I affect to work, but her presence overpowers me.

"Buenos noces," I say.

She smiles shyly, nods, continues to concentrate on her work.

Who knows what rivers she has crossed, what deserts she has suffered, what the details of her life must be. I am interested in these things, would like to know how much education she has, in what circumstances she lives in this fatally expensive city, why she is not in school. But these are also details of no consequence. I am in thrall to her, wrapped in her delicate drapery, fixated on the absurd smoothness of her arms, her high forehead, her glass clean eyes.

I look down at my indenture of trust, weighty stuff indeed, feel the gabardine in my trouser leg shift as I contemplate throwing myself on my knees before her, before a penniless cleaning girl, for no good reason.

"Finish, sir," she declares and wheels her cart from the room.

Resistance is futile. One might as well stand in a Borgian case with the android Data, a tube in one's head, another attached to one's privates.

The day would end, the office close, and I would be cast from my daily charade as unceremoniously as a drunk from a saloon. I would take the train to the rooming house knowing that as I walked in the front door, into my room, there would be only silence, myself, my thoughts, my possessions, not much else until mercifully Monday again crept up on me. I might dawdle at the grocers, browse in the bookstore, but eventually, always, eventually I would have to go home, through the hall, up the stairs, to my room, to hours of nothing.

It hardly matters now but I could list, if I had the heart to, the steps I took to derail this sameness, the committees I joined in support of the museum and the orchestra, the art classes and the poetry readings I attended in the hope that perhaps by sheer force of will I might break out of this cycle, find an opening and barrel right through it to the light outside. I sat for hours in coffee shops purporting to drink, to read, smiling, making small comments, clearing a space at my table in the hope that someone might see fit to join me, but it was as if I scarcely existed. The acknowledgments I received (and how gory must this be?) were cursory, my attempts awkward. Sometimes it felt as if I were waiting for lightning to strike, and how great were the chances of that? There were other things a more creative man might have found to try, I am sure, but in the end, rather than be seen to disadvantage I chose not to be seen at all.

Each night then as I brushed my teeth, combed what was left of my hair, I would look in the mirror and wonder whether it was that alone, the features I was seeing, and not something else, that accounted for my isolation. If I were not so plain, perhaps, my other flaws, my inability to make others warm to me, might be less of a handicap.

But both are my features and both, it seems, are immutable. The process of natural selection had set in stone that mine was a strain destined to wither. Is it any surprise that at the nub of it all there is the blush of sexual indiscretion? Loneliness in men, after all, tends to acquire a sexual tinge, does it not?

—∞∞—

The room in which I lived was in an old clapboard house, slightly tilted, painted blue. It has been torn down now, replaced by a brick building with a coffee shop on the first floor and office suites on the second, but as I recall back then it held about a half dozen tenants in all. It was very cheap indeed.

Rebecca lived in the room between mine and the bathroom. I used to wonder about her, who she was, what she did with herself, and occasionally when I passed her I would be tempted to say something, to attempt an acquaintance. I did not. Better, I remember thinking, to leave the place at which I lived free of my usual red-eared awkwardness.

When we did speak it was she who initiated it, not I. She stopped me one morning on the stairs.

"The landlady says you're a lawyer," she said, more an assertion, an accusation even, than a question.

"She speaks the truth," I replied, aware of how I must sound, unable to sound differently.

She stood for a moment in silence, surveying me, a look of distaste on her face.

"I need to talk to a lawyer," she said after a pause.

She was a tall woman, affected a Bohemian way of dressing. I told her I was in a hurry but that we could talk later.

"This won't take long," she had insisted and begun to tell her story.

I interrupted her.

"I am indisposed," I told her, and began edging away. "I have business elsewhere."

"Sheesh," I heard her say to my back. "Who talks like that?"

It wasn't until several nights later, and long after I had gone to bed, that she knocked on my door. I was in my pajamas but that did not deter her and she came into the room without waiting to be invited. Once in she strode across to the window and then, finding no chair, sat on the edge of my bed and began describing a problem I remember only because it was a typical Rebecca tangle involving several people and an implausible set of circumstances. She looked annoyed when I told her that there wasn't much I could do for her. I wasn't about to jeopardize my position at Henshaw & Potter by pursuing some quixotic venture for which we would surely never recover our fees.

"But you're a lawyer," she kept insisting, as if that should be the end of it all.

I'm not sure exactly why, but I do associate Rebecca, and strongly, with the disjointed, almost unhinged, character of those early years. She was an artist of sorts, not the kind who paints pictures, but rather an itinerant poster-maker who eked out a living chalking restaurant specials on blackboards and painting things like aubergines for a collection of small supermarkets. She would leave each morning with her folio case and pastels, make her various stops, return to the boarding house each evening with inky fingers and often a small supply of vegetables that she would sometimes take in payment. Perhaps it was the contrast, her careless, unbridled sexuality that made her presence so intrusive. Her lack of modesty, for instance, allowed her to barge into my room wrapped only in a towel, or, in the middle of a sentence, without pausing, to pull off a brassiere through her sleeve, even as I paid dearly, dreamed of, pined for, the chance to see, to touch, a willing partner.

Sometimes Rebecca would make herself comfortable on my bed, her hands behind her head, and relate details of her sexual life as if I were a confidant, a female friend, hardly a man at all.

"You wouldn't understand," she would say, a knee raised, a thigh exposed, and I would respond, "I suppose one wouldn't."

She entertained a string of lovers in her room—I would encounter them coming from the bathroom, one of her towels invariably draped around their necks—and they would nod as they passed in a casual manner as if I were a mere table in the hallway, not much more than a number on a door.

When they'd left, as often as not, she'd drift into my room to talk.

"Did you see that asshole Jerry?" she might ask.

"Tall fellow with the chin?" I might say.

"He's a pig," she would say. "A disgusting, disgusting pig."

"Why is that?" I might ask.

41

"Never you mind," she would answer. "Just take my word for it."

"So why do you allow him to keep coming back?" I would ask, and here she would break into a mischievous smile, as if the answer were self-evident: "He has his moments," she might say.

For all my supposed nonchalance as I listened to her stories, my shows of solidarity, sometimes when I heard her voice in the hallway, I would crouch at the keyhole and try to catch a glimpse of her as she meandered — involved in conversation and scarcely covered — from the bathroom to her room.

"So how can he be both appealing and disgusting?' I would ask.

"You wouldn't even know what I was talking about," she replied.

Living under one roof at such proximity makes a certain kind of intimacy inevitable. There are power outages that draw you to a single candle in a dark hallway, lost keys, trivial common experiences like failed heat and broken pipes. With Rebecca too there were instances when I found her sitting crying outside her own door, once when I heard such angry shouting coming from her room that I was tempted to knock and ask if all was well. Rebecca was one of those people whose lives are a flurry of loose ends, the kind that constantly threaten to pull the whole fabric of the thing apart — violent lovers, angry creditors, drunken siblings.

"I'm not here," she'd whisper, crouched behind my door, her hand on the key. From down the hall we'd hear banging on her door, her name called over and over.

"Who is he?" I'd ask.

"My father," she might say, or, "My cousin Billy. He's not so bad, really."

For the rest of it, our way of doing things arose from Rebecca having almost no money and I somewhat more. So she would wander in at dinnertime, or enlist my help with her laundry, and it was always I who supplied the quarters or the food, bought the tickets, paid the taxi. In the end, perhaps inevitably, Rebecca was the first woman with whom I was intimate and with whom there was not also some commercial agreement. *(Well, as I have already intimated, in the interests of accuracy I may need to rephrase that.)* Rebecca was the first woman who undertook to have sexual intercourse with me without being paid to do so, and who approached the act with a full awareness of what she was doing. There was no sidling up, no vagueness, no fumbling. *(Later, please.)*

Simply stated, one night as she was lying on my bed having told another man to leave her own, with one hand lost somewhere in her nightgown, she invited me to make love to her.

"Alfie," she said simply. "Do you want me to do you?"

I remember wondering if I could be right in understanding her as I did. I remember looking at her with dread, crossing the room to close the window, locking the door, fastening the curtains with a safety pin. I thought it oddly ironic that underneath the mattress on which she was lying, like a pea beneath a princess, was my carefully selected cache of pornography. *(I preferred images of plain girls, I should add, always on their backs like pinned frogs and receiving what they did with surprised patience.)*

She had a long, sinewy body, calloused feet, bent her knees as I approached.

I will take the opportunity to shift into something equally distasteful, my tentative little excursions, acts of depredation that I myself found as contemptible as they were irresistible. *(You see, of course, how steep the prissiness still runs. Even with Nok's presence in the air I prance and prittle about this, about paying for time in rooms with wet towels on chairs, walking along certain half-deserted streets that were, in fact, dangerous, and onto which I would never as my daylight self have dreamed of venturing after dark.)* I was no virgin the night Rebecca tendered herself to me. Pardon me if I have given another impression. I am all that I have said I am, but

I am also more, and less as well. One is driven to do this absurd act by genetic impulses, or so they tell me in late night documentaries. (My reading habits do not extend to such matters.)

There are rules to be followed in such ventures. (*I try to be honest, but I am not comfortable with anatomy, quite unsure, given the circumstances, what of this is gratuitous and what relevant.*) There is always a bed, of course, a range of cleanliness to be found in the sheets and other furnishings of one-night cheap hotels, a flowerpot or two. One wonders about that, about the objective in it, why this business venue is arranged as it is. The women either tender themselves for undress or in a single gesture slip from their clothes. There is a period of patience during which one may touch, marvel at the license in it, but that is always brief. Penetration is expected, completion is hastened. Often this is done in complete silence and when sounds are made, they are practiced and patently insincere. (Why would anyone mistake such sounds for honest pleasure? Are there men deluded enough to believe it?)

Occasionally afterwards, as one dresses, pulls one's outfit together in a series of hasty jerks, there is conversation.

"You got a wife?" one may be asked.

"Heavens no."

"Where you from? You have an accent."

"England."

It may stop there. It may not. Once a girl says, "You're a nice guy. What're you coming here for?" But the answer is so complex, so elusive, so obvious, one cannot attempt it even if one were so inclined. It is all ridiculous, no? If I could have worn a mask, said nothing, I would have preferred it.

I was also cheated, touched as if contaminated, brushed off with contempt.

"Get the fuck out of here before I bust your ugly-ass face," a woman yells after refusing to do what she has been paid to.

(*The blood drains from me as I recount this. I stand rock-still, outraged, Alfred Buber out of his element, in his element, overwhelmed by thoughts of police, of bruises, of Arthur Henshaw. I gather my belongings, swallow the bile, leave hurriedly. I wither with embarrassment to think of it, let alone to repeat it, but I have committed to be honest. Star Log 5725, in the month of Sivan. So it happened.)*

"What are you always thinking about?" Rebecca once asked over cartons of Chinese food.

"Nothing in particular," I answered.

"I have a feeling," Rebecca said, "that one day I'm going to come home and you're going to have vanished without a trace."

In a way, of course, that was exactly what I was counting on. I would stand and daydream amidst the piles of cement and boxes of tile until well into the evening.

⚬⚬⚬

Would you like to know how I met Nok?

(You will say: How can you tell this to me, to me of all persons, how can you? And the answer: I do not know.)

She is on the floor, on her knees, between my legs. Someone has handed her a little basket. In it are tissues, a bottle of mouthwash, a bottle of Johnson's baby oil. The basket has a picture of a cat taped to the side. What she is doing feels good. Although there are others in the room, two Australian men being hustled to my left, other girls, no one pays too close attention.

I am not shamed, not embarrassed, intrigued rather, quite overcome with the newness and the daring. I lean back and wonder at this, at the girl between my legs. I feel a little sorry for her as she turns to the side to exchange a comment with a friend, gets back to work, does not appear at all touched by shame or particularly in need of privacy for what everything else in my life has told me is a private act. I am not happy to be mastering her in this way, to have her bowed before me, but there is something brutally honest in it too, something terribly naked in the exchange. Buber is not for these moments a chaste cipher, untouched, untouchable, in the shadows.

45

One of the girls kneels on the bench and begins to rub my shoulders as the other, intent on her mission, remains there, her head bobbing, crouched on the floor.

The place is *(now how does one put it without being too crass, how does one say it without putting too fine a point on it? Such places exist)* a bar in a country far away, but of course it is more than that. Outside the sidewalk is dirty, strewn with half-empty food cartons and cigarette ends, and the air reeks of charcoal smoke and incense, dried squid, who knows what unspeakable else. People yell, solicit, argue in hoarse tones. I have stumbled in and sat down, and without fanfare a young woman has positioned herself cross-legged on the floor, and once settled has begun to undo my belt as if she were readying some piece of equipment, and I have not stopped her.

"Feel good?" she asks.

I nod.

"Good," she repeats, and then, as if I had not myself noticed, the girl on the bench adds, "She suck you."

"Yes, lass," I murmur, Scottie at the helm. "So she does."

Back in my hotel room I will examine my skin carefully to confirm that the filth remains on the inside, has not erupted as I fear it eventually must, to the surface. *(Eventually it will spill over, of course, and then by my own volition.)*

The girl on the floor, the one who when her task is completed will melt away into the reaches of the bar carrying her wicker basket, is Nok.

———

Let me describe Arthur Henshaw, one of the firm's founders and its leading figure until I, Alfred the Buber, moved into his chair. He is very tall, unnervingly tall, and almost inhumanly polished. Sometimes, especially in the early days, I would wonder how it was possible to be, always and without lapse, so flawless in appearance, so perfectly pressed, to have silvery hair that is never out of place and manners that are unremittingly courtly.

"I notice," he once said, "that you give your address as a post office box. Where exactly is it that you live?"

"I'm in the process of building," I answered. "West of the city."

"I see," Henshaw replied. "Good thinking to get a box. Assures continuity. I wouldn't have thought of it."

"It does make things simpler," I agreed.

I attended all of the firm's functions in those days, torturous though they invariably were, was appropriate, cordial, punctual, and of course, always alone.

"You're one of the new fellows," Harold Potter said to me shortly before he died.

"Yes," I said.

I had met him a dozen times. The ragged quality of his memory was one of those things everyone in the firm knew about but nobody mentioned.

"You should get a wife," he had said. "Every young lawyer should get a wife. It takes care of a lot of distractions."

"I'm sure I will, Mr. Potter," I had assured him.

"That's the spirit," he said, touching my shoulder. "There's someone for each of us, take my word."

"You always leave before we have a chance to visit with each other," Henshaw's wife, appropriately named Grace, once observed. "I shall make a point of cornering you early next time."

"I'm sorry," I apologized. "It's my own fault for trying to fit too much into an evening."

"I envy you, you know," she said. "Youth is everything."

Of course I had no other commitments. Far from it. I would leave, walk to my car, drive around for a while, eventually head to the smelly rooms and dark places that constituted the filth of my underlife. From that to this in a heartbeat, from cocktail plates and crystal glasses to threadbare towels and the stink of stale tobacco.

From the rustle of evening dresses to the dull pang that accompanies a thought of mottled skin under lamplight.

Those who know me would say that I am a censorious man, intolerant of stupidity, at times overly stern. I am told that the young clerks at Henshaw & Potter tended to stay away from my assignments, preferred those that would be less carefully scrutinized, less likely to be returned with red circles around split infinitives and run-on sentences. There is more than one person who must be rejoicing at the collapse of my reputation, but I would have to say that when the present scandal broke in all its searing immediacy, to my own great surprise there was no shame left in me at all.

You see, my dearest, it seems to have all seeped out over the years, to have neutralized itself with itself, to have ground itself into a heap of meaningless dust. The more of it there is, the more debasing it is, the less it matters.

———— ∞ ————

It was the night Henshaw called me in to let me know that the firm had decided to promote me to partnership that something deep within me changed. From there one can trace a line directly to the nightmare in which I now find myself.

Henshaw was, as usual, assiduously polite, complimentary, even grateful.

"Your years at the firm have been exceptional ones," I remember him saying. "Your judgment and maturity are a credit to you and an important asset of this firm."

He sat for a while in my office and reminisced about the firm's past, about the practice of law when he was a young man, about other things, and all along I sat behind my desk trying to assimilate what had happened. *We are peers now, I remember thinking, this silver-haired scion and I, partners in the same firm, and yet still I am in awe of him, tongue-tied, incomplete.*

"I expect," he said as he stood at the door, "that a young blade like yourself probably has plans to paint the town tonight. If I were any younger I would insist on joining you."

"I'll do what I can to keep the firm's name out of the newspapers, Art," I said.

"Now I'm tempted," Henshaw had responded with a smile.

I was relieved, to be sure, but there wasn't much excitement in it. I called Nigel and he was gracious enough, invited me for dinner over the weekend. I had a small car by then, remember sitting in it outside the rooming house and looking up at the dark windows of my room, eventually going in, taking off my suit, eating a sandwich, reading Wallace Stegner's *The Spectator Bird*. I like Stegner's old codger protagonists, how he builds them little worlds in which they function with autonomy. Someone is generally crippled in some way too, able to slow things down and to make life more meticulous. I must say, very much against my wishes, I had become a spectator bird myself.

An hour or two later I put my Stegner aside and left the building. I remember walking down the street and sitting on a bench, experiencing the overwhelming sensation that I had almost completed the task of cementing myself like a corpse into a wall. I had done everything I believed I ought to do, had been industrious, careful, diligent, and yet all of it, the gentility, the formal manners, had become as stifling as a shroud, an invention, a character devised for a performance to which I was wedded more resolutely than to any woman. I had thought that with time I would become resigned to my fate, but I had not, and far from it. I was not a sterile hermit content to putter about his days, there in a frigid law office, here in my solitary cell.

I wanted more, even if it was more than I was entitled to.

Is it then such a crime that I perpetrated, such a black deception, were my expeditions so extraordinary as to place me completely beyond the pale of acceptable human conduct? My old mentor would say that they were, but he had the choice to live out his life ensconced in his late father's manor house, was a smug man, beautifully tailored, exceptionally elegant (though even he, in the end, turned out to have feet of clay). But back then all I could conjure was his wife's silver hair, his graceful daughter, his Great Danes racing about the lawn before his house. He must have wakened each morning with a sense of calm and assurance, he *must* have, being able to charm as he did, to engage a woman's attention, to be looked at with dipped eyelids, to provoke restless fingers. I, on the other hand, am a speck in a white suit, a blob in a barnyard standing on a mound of filth.

This is, though, a large planet with many things on it. What some acquire with charm, an easy manner, a handsome, aquiline face, in carpeted rooms and landscaped gardens, I will acquire elsewhere and using a quite different currency.

Those who have known me for years at Henshaw & Potter would doubt the truth of it.

"Buber," they would exclaim. "Our Buber? You have the wrong chap."

I have no doubt of it.

There is no shame in it, though I am shamed by it.

You will ask, doubtless, how you cross the bridge from this to that, from the daily regimen of longing and tawdry excursion to that, a full-fledged, fully conscious expedition to beyond the pale.

I do not know. I do not know how the idea of finding beauty among the poor of the Orient began, what caused this notion to infiltrate my dreams until the thought of it became a constant refuge. What role memories of Rosalind may have played I cannot say (it does seem rather obvious, one would think, too obvious, too self-indulgent). Nor can I explain what led me to collect the advertisements you will find in my desk drawer, the ones in which men are offered Asian wives of surpassing demureness. I do know this. Before any of it began, before even the thought of it, one day over lunch I heard Arthur Henshaw remark that he had once been in a city with the most beautiful young women on earth and that most of them were available "without shame, without self-consciousness, for a song." He said it lightly, laughingly, depicted himself as floating above a sea of temptation. It will not come as a surprise that the place he described became my destination.

∽∞∼

I did not set out solely in pursuit of sexual adventure. I am almost sure of this. It was never the grunting and the panting of it, the grubby little details, that drove me, not the pubis and the mons, to be Buberesque about it, that were the draw. It was always something else, something far more elusive.

Nok herself was bewildered, at first, back in the beginning.

(Buber holds her narrow brown foot in the air as she lies on the bed under a single sheet, traces the curve of her calf with his finger. What is it, what, I obsess, about this slender curve, this smooth brown muscle, that holds me so entranced? It cannot be lust alone. I have had her, recently, cannot penetrate her again and grab any further pleasure in it, and yet this curve, this calf, holds me still, dominates me, entrances me beyond description. Or the hardness at the back of her thigh, the very fine, almost imperceptible follicles that give texture to the skin. I run a finger there and I want it too, endlessly, for myself. I have her, for a pittance, for today, for tomorrow, for a week or a month if I choose, and yet that is not enough.

She is polite, methodical, wholly detached.

I have never been so close to such beauty, at liberty to touch such limbs as often and wherever and however I choose, and yet doing so is jarring because it is especially clear to me how unaffected she remains, how far I am from possessing any part of her that is important to her. She does this because she must, and with a grace that comes from deep within and cannot be feigned, and yet she is hardly with me at all.

That is not enough. Of course that is not enough. It makes the need more urgent still. Is this all, could it be, primeval sludge talking, imperatives so base they defy description? Is that it, nothing more?

She turns over.

51

"What you do?" she asks as I hold her leg, still, in the air. "Why you do that?"

Why indeed? We are still in that hotel, that provincial hotel near her home. I have been ill but am recovered enough to travel. She has tended to me in my illness with kindness and dedication. What else it is I need from her I cannot say. I am driven to it, must have it, must do it, must be here, and yet there is no end in sight, no satisfaction, no joy. I lean over, sink my face into her. The scent of her is sweet, inimitable, like nothing else I have inhaled.

"What you do?" she asks again. "What you want?"

"Everything," I say, and her English, tenuous at best, is not complete enough to follow. "I want everything and nothing at all."

"You have paid father," she says. "Now I stay with you."

Let me be clear about something. I am, in my heart, an old man. Lurching desires are a thing of the past. I am no longer driven by the urges that swept me about in my twenties and thirties. I am in thrall to something quite different and far more elusive. What I want is not the abductor minus, the flexor longus, the vastus lateralis – *these are of no conceivable interest* – and yet they are of all-consuming interest.)

So there you have it, the asymmetry, the obsession with anatomy that flies in the face of my knowledge, my certainty, that virtue comes from within.

I cannot quite describe how it was to make those first, tentative plans, to edge towards an expedition that was as impossible as it was inevitable. I would stand in my office, the phone ringing on my desk, my secretary bustling in and out, and all I could think of was how absurd it was that this sober pillar, this drone, should be contemplating a race halfway around the world to no honorable purpose.

I don't know now, now that it has ended as it has, what I was thinking as I barreled on with one detail after another. Perhaps my private inventory of disasters awaiting me—an accident somewhere, a heart attack to knock all sense out of me on some filthy street, a murder, my body dumped in a putrid canal—were simply my better self telling me to stay home, to let it be, to live with what I had.

"Alfred Buber," someone, recognizing me, will call from across a crowded street. "What on earth are *you* doing here?"

I will feign confusion at this apparent resemblance to a person I am not: "He was in Paris at the time," they will be told.

"I could have sworn it was him. How many people look like Buber?"

"Mercifully."

"Mercifully. But really. It must have been Buber, even the voice: *'No habla Inglaise.'* "

Or I could brazen it out. Try this: "Half-way round the world," I will exclaim. "What a coincidence."

"What are you doing here?" I will be asked.

"I was in Paris, got bored, jumped on a plane and ended up here, but to tell you the truth I'm delighted to see someone familiar. This place is putting my self-restraint to the test."

"You?" they'd say. "We can't imagine you not being in control."

Haw haw, Buber you scoundrel. Nobody's fool but his own.

———

In some respects I am not a practical person. The design of my house—not yet completed at that time but filled now with white carpeting, translucent walls, floors of stone so cold some rooms cannot be heated—bears this out. In other respects, of course, I am obsessive in my need for order, and in planning my transgression I was determined to leave nothing to chance. Rebecca, large and immovable there on her back watching my every move, was the only impediment, the only person who would even notice I was not where I should have been.

"I think I'm going to go away for a week or two," I may have said to her.

"Alone?" came her answer.

"I think so."

"Not together? I could use a holiday."

"I would like some time alone."

"Where are you going?"

"Paris," I said.

"Why Paris?"

"For the food and the art," I must have said, and Rebecca, without any sense of the irony of it, asked: "How can you go somewhere like that without me?"

Even with the perspective of distance—perhaps especially with the perspective of distance—I cannot say what I believed I was doing, what specifically I expected to find. Perhaps it was simply a sexual adventure after all, nothing more, a dark grab at what I had not been worthy of finding more subtly; or perhaps buried beneath the artifice were thoughts that I might actually find someone, some person at last, someone naive and beautiful, rescue her from poverty, bring her back to be my wife, to live under the withering scrutiny of my relatives and colleagues.

A heroic quest then. Bubador the Troubadour.

—∞∞—

My housekeeper has left for the day, has finished tidying rooms she makes no secret she finds strange, hateful even, and returned in a smoking Chevrolet to her husband in the city. It is just me in this room, me and Nigel, my imagination's scathing critic, me and thoughts of my genteel former partner, Arthur Henshaw. For fleeting moments, incredibly even now when it is all said and done, I fret over what they would think of Nok; but then perhaps the old men would surprise me by the mildness of their response. At times it is not them but the young women at Henshaw & Potter, the ones who have walked admiringly through my house, sensible women in whose view of the world I see a great deal to admire, who intrude most starkly. They would be quick to pass judgment, these liberated souls who take a stern view of so many things. They would say that Nok is just another absurdity, more

absurd even than I am, perhaps that she needs protection from me,
that they cannot contemplate viewing it any other way.

And they would be partly right, would they not? I may always
have seemed to them, as indeed at times I seem to myself, the kind
of aloof, marginal man one suspects of oddity.

Maybe Nok is, when all is said and done, simply a symptom
of wickedness, a malady.

———

And so, without further ado, it is time to flagellate myself,
to talk about the fiasco of that first expedition. Pardon me if
I do so in Buberesque fashion. Reserved men, as I say, shy
men at heart who lack adventure and spirit, who lack heat
and dread the slap of rejection, the sneer of failure, tend to
recount moments of spittle and slime, if they must, from a
distance, to do it with a show of disinterest and with a measure of irony and showy intellect thrown in for good measure. Especially to an audience that includes a daughter.

These things, these things I must tell you, dearest,
dearest, are such things. Forgive the vamping. It is bound
up with me. You will follow the kernels, my Gretel.

Ahem.

Eventually, then, one of the ten-day periods I have
blocked out on my calendar approaches, and I find myself
in an airline ticket office holding a seat for Paris and then
on to Asia. It is almost, as I begin to make my plans, as if I
do so Hansel and Gretel-like, leaving tiny bits in the trail for
someone diligent and resourceful to follow. I pay cash for
my ticket and misspell my name so that a computer search
will not find me (Mr. Beber is booked to the brothels of Asia.
He lives in the same town as your Mr. Buber, this Beber, and
his telephone number is eerily similar though not the same.)
That month my telephone bill would in fact confirm two
calls to a hotel making reservations for this same Mr. Beber,
reservations I would not entrust to a travel agent who might
have suspected my motives. I purport to pack for a European winter but instead I pack for a tropical summer, lay
sweaters on the bed for Rebecca if she cares to notice, but

fold linen trousers carefully into my bag. I remember being plagued by a sense that I was pulling free of my moorings, doing something beyond unwise, beyond reckless, and yet I was powerless to stop any of it.

Henshaw had added, unwittingly of course, a trace of almost hysterical unreality to this illicit little trip.

"There's this magnificent little place on the quai de Tournelle," he had said. "Grace and I go there every time we're in Paris. In fact, mention our name. The maitre d' knows us." And I had dutifully noted it in a little book, the restaurants and pensions I would not be within a continent of, the out-of-the-way galleries, the cloistered vineyards that would supposedly be considered for this impeccable itinerary.

"Here," he had said the morning before I left. "Grace took the liberty of writing down some of our favorite spots for you, and a few other suggestions too. Don't feel bad if you don't take her up on any of them, but she does like you and rather enjoyed compiling it."

"Thank you so much," I said, ashamed to be misleading her so cruelly, to have made her embark on such a fool's errand. I pictured her at her little tea desk scanning her diary for suggestions while all along only I know that she was wasting her time, that her careful little notes would sit unread in my suitcase.

I boarded a plane and at that moment I was who I was, Alfred Buber, attorney-at-law, soon to be a partner at Henshaw & Potter, casually but carefully dressed, on a well-earned trip to Paris to sample the rich food and art of Europe. And then the plane touched down at Orly airport and I prepared to slough myself. I pulled down over my ears an L.L.Bean hat I had bought for the occasion — I think they call it an Irish walking hat or some such thing — polished my sunglasses, placed them on my ample nose.

I remember glancing at myself in an airport mirror. The round little satyr looked like nothing so much as a well-fed Irish spy — that, or a Jewish farmer with eye ache.

Along with any other transgressions for which I might be responsible, in Paris I was a relatively short flight from my mother's little flat in London.

"We haven't seen each other for years and you didn't think to try and see me," she might have said, settling back into one of the Queen Anne chairs she'd had shipped "home" from Salisbury. "You might have telephoned."

I had seen her flat in Golders Green only once, shortly after I began work at Henshaw & Potter. After that, what with the penury I brought upon myself in order to build my house and my increasing responsibilities, visiting England had been something I kept in mind to do but never actually did. We were never close, my mother and I, though we did write to each other from time to time as the occasion warranted. I get some of my formality from her, I think. When she married my father her family disowned her because he was a Jew and a Communist, but apparently they're reconciled now. When I met them on that one trip they were all perfectly polite to me, but in the end they made me feel a little like the product of some indiscretion on my mother's part rather than a relative. It's rather strange to be treated that way by people with whom you share blood.

As I understand it, my mother settled into her role as staid English widow just as she was a perfectly adequate Rhodesian housewife. She is a little like a chameleon in that way, I would say, only more passive. I have no idea what she lives on since the old man couldn't have believed in insurance. If she had ever needed help in any respect, I'd have been sure to provide it.

"Alfred's done very well for himself," I'm sure she would once have said if asked. "He's never married, but he's quite settled in his ways. I'm sure he's making the most of things."

—⚬⚬⚬—

When I should have been checking into the Montparnasse Park Hotel, I was securely belted into a 747 and on my way, flying high above the Balkans, Turkey, who knows

57

where else; and then finally, wearily, I watched through a window as the plane taxied across a stretch of tar and approached the glowing terminal of my destination. It was something out of a disjointed dream, but equally clearly it was no dream at all.

I, Alfred Buber, had cobbled together this trip across the world on a vague and illicit search, and now it was underway and there was no denying any of it. It would have been my first day of sightseeing in Paris, a pointless, uninteresting exercise fraught with the same inadequacies, the same incompleteness, the same emptiness. I would sooner have been in a coma than staring at art and guzzling pastries in Paris.

And yet, no sooner had I set foot on the ground, than I would rather have been anywhere else than where I was.

———

How much more before I get to what happened on that trip, what has upended everything?

This, then.

The airport has a distinctive fragrance. Probably it is only the filtered air of a conditioner battling against a soup-like humidity, but it has also the musty aroma of unpacked crates, fresh cement, stale incense, unopened bottles of perfume. As I step across the creamy tiles, pass the checkpoints, undergo the formalities, I have a sense that I have slipped through a tear in the fabric of my own history and emerged at a place without reference points. The same has happened, on occasion, to the starship Enterprise; it slips through the space-time continuum, you see, and ends up in places that have no relation to where it has been or where it is going.

———

It is three in the morning when I finally climb into a taxi and we take off into the empty street. There is a shrine on the car's dashboard, lace decorations around its windows.

"First time here, sir?" the driver asks.

"Oh no," I answer, and it is not truthful, of course, but what can such things as truth matter now?

"Very hot," he says, and I agree that it is.

"Business or pleasure," he presses on and I suddenly create a slice of my new *persona*, one born of nothing other than artifice and an empty need to dissemble.

"Both," I say. "I live in Singapore and come here quite a bit."

Who knows why I say it, where it even comes from, whether he buys it.

"Singapore very expensive," he says.

The road is straight and broad but spotted with bumps. Every so often the aging Toyota goes over a pothole the size of a wheelbarrow and shoots up into the air, lands with a jolt.

"Very expensive," I say.

"Expensive here too," he says.

We pass an open truck with a man sleeping on its bed, his legs dangling over the side in a way that elsewhere would provoke a police stop in a heartbeat, pass white-washed skyscrapers, temples of impossible intricacy, a panoply of colorful billboards. In the air the smell of old fruit, of a river with lilies rotting on its banks, of charcoal and diesel fumes, lingers like a veil. As we approach my hotel, the driver points casually to one side and says, "Many ladies here, sir," and I, assuming the *persona* of my fastidious little story about business in Singapore, ignore him, let it pass as if it has no relevance to me. It is, of course, why I have chosen this hotel, *because* it is on the verge of the world-famous road, but now this priapic bluestocking receives the information with distaste.

I allow a world-weary, sour expression to creep across my dissolute face.

"Many beautiful ladies," he repeats and I say, dismissively, condescendingly: "So they say."

"You like?" he asks and I ignore him. "Beautiful girl help you sleep better."

We draw up to the hotel and a man in an ornate helmet opens the door. The driver, however, has not quite given up.

"Tomorrow I take you good place," he says. "Many beautiful ladies."

I ignore him, but fathom this, if you will. Fathom this. The irrepressible Buber has come across the world in search of beautiful ladies to help him sleep better, but now that this is on offer he treats the man with disdain, will not even hear him out. There is hostility in my manner, an edge, as I say, of distaste. The adherence to character, a rickety construct of a character, moreover, built over the years of frustration and loneliness, takes me by surprise. *That* Buber, our stuffy, rigid prig of a Buber, is in France, is he not, snuffling about in some loathsome museum or other. *This* Buber, our Beber of a Buber, is an adventurer, is supposed to be quite different. What the devil was the point of it, if not?

The intrusion is strange and unexpected, threatens to make a mockery of everything.

"I give you card," the man presses on as he opens the trunk.

"No," I say firmly, drawing back and leaving him with the card in his hand.

Oh boy, does this Beber Buber, waddling off into the lobby, ever deserve what he gets.

Let me press on with this to its inevitable conclusion.

It is a hotel room like all others, the fabrics perhaps more ornate, on one wall posters of things that would not be usual elsewhere: women in tiered headdress performing dances, strange dragons. The porter walks around opening doors and drapes, points to a basket with rambutan fruit and to the laundry bags—lingers, in short.

"Please," I said, anxious to be alone, and hand him his tip.

The door closes and I am filled again with the sense that I am in a dream gone wrong; not a nightmare as such, but merely a dream that has become too unshakeable, too intangible, without even the lining of escape with which dreams are usually cloaked.

⸺∞⸺

I wake up late, disoriented. "What *are* you doing?" I ask myself as I shave. But then as I come down into the lobby and smell the strange fragrances, eat a breakfast served by waitresses with orchids in their hair and gold bangles at their wrists, something returns. I will keep going. I must. As I step into the blinding sunlight, the iron ball of remorse that had been clanking along behind me suddenly becomes as light as air. There are dangers in it, all sorts of ambiguities, yes, but my life is not some pristine thing encased in crystal to be protected against all exposure. There is nothing pure left in me to be tainted, nothing so foul as to be forever banished from my thoughts.

(I see a cloud crossing Nigel's face as he hears me think this. Well, relax. In seventy hours I will turn around and run, tail between my legs, an unsatiated, insatiable satyr.)

There is a gauntlet of taxi drivers, a hectic street, smoking air, beetling three-wheeled samlors, shouts, gusts of dusty wind, the wheedling of hawkers. There is a thumping sun, crowds of people, temples with crimson trim, armies of gold Buddhas, an opaque river thick with refuse and vegetation. I notice the women, of course. Of course I notice the women. They are slim and dark with a chaste, slithering walk and faces that radiate delicacy even as they swelter in the heat, step across puddles, pick through patches of melting tar.

"American?" the touts call. "Where you go? I take you."

I walk up the street and down a narrow alley, look in windows, cross an overpass, order a dish of noodles, leave it untouched. I do not stray far, am never more than ten minutes from my hotel as I walk in slow, great, elliptic loops.

Pathetic, isn't it?

Each time I circle back and cross the dark and famous street, long and gray and pitted with puddles and bits of blowing paper, muddy gutters, upended tables, women swabbing the floors of empty bars. I know that within hours

61

it will come to life and that while I pretend to walk about like a tourist, to sample this, to gawk at that, the tenure of this gritty, intrepid little tourist is limited. Buber the thruster, the womanizer, awaits only the cover of the dark.

I can't help thinking of my mother, there in her floral-patterned rocking chair in Golders Green: "I mean Alfred. What are you doing there? What on earth?"

Or worse, Nigel's unique brand of scorn: "A sorry sight, indeed. Schlepping oneself across the world in search of desperate women. Is it more than that, Alfred? Could it ever be?"

<hr/>

When night falls the world-famous street takes on its real life, one filled with lights and music and slim girls showing their legs in doorways, and it calls to mind something of everything, of adolescent afternoons, of nights spent day-dreaming, of my rooming house with its moth-eaten carpet. I stand and ponder as the touts spread the promise that for a pittance, just through the arch, up several stairs, a man can have his choice of a thousand dancers, pick from tiers of girls sitting demurely behind glass windows, indulge any desire one can imagine in the anonymity of strange-ness. Ten steps up from the sidewalk, towards the music, away from the smells of cooking, the laughs, the grinning boys, the poor of the Orient, beauty in all its forms, at long last, awaits. Men pause, listen, weigh the offers, disappear into dark rooms and then return arm in arm with girls who pause to make silent obeisance to a garlanded Buddha, do it without a glimmer of reticence while Buber, who has trav-eled across the world to be here, is immobilized by a host of reservations. The threat of disease alone overwhelms him, and then beyond the disease, that some of these girls are here against their will; and that it is all so raucous and so commercial and so vulgar, and that there is so much that is wrong in it, and what would they say and what should I say, and it all floods in to drown any vestige of desire until I find myself just standing, a spectacle, unable to go backwards, unable to go forwards, perfectly stuck. Oh Buber, what a clown, not one with the law students, not one with his law partners, not one with the townspeople in the village, not one now either.

And such a harsh critic too. Disgusting men, he thinks, so smug in taking what they are not entitled to have, in possessing what should not be theirs to possess, a disgrace to all of us, these aging monsters and the lithe, giggling, animated things on their arms. They cling, look up appreciatively, have smooth legs, honey-colored legs that clip along like colts, crimped little waists, delicate shoulders. *(You see, I don't need to be punished for my transgressions. I do an adequate job of it myself.)* One way or another, I neither leave nor go in, approach, step away, circle the block, up one road, down another, along a third. *(That's our Buber for you. Stings like a butterfly, hovers like a bee.)*

I return to the hotel. I am the only man in recorded history, it seems, unable to consummate a deal here, even here, have set some sort of record, one noted by the hotel guard waiting to sign in the girls other men bring back as he opens the door and tips his helmet. As I ride the elevator I think of my colleagues putting their children to bed in Dover and Newton, reading *Peter Rabbit* to babies in flannel pajamas, contemplating cups of coffee before fires in living rooms filled with photographs.

The touts' calls echo like a mockery.

I dream, ironically, of Rebecca, more, that I am in love with her.

"How can you go to Paris without me?' she had asked, and now it does seem cruel that I have done this. We *could* have stayed at the Montparnasse Park Hotel, walked along the Seine, eaten croissants, drunk wine out of pitchers. I would have made her laugh, created something romantic. All of a sudden her clumsiness, the sense that I could disappear and that she would scarcely notice, shrinks, and instead I see love in what we have, something faithful and painfully open. I have missed her truest charm, her candor, her disingenuousness, an honesty buried somewhere under the layers of chaos and vagueness. I resolve, lying in the darkness on the eighth floor, fitfully asleep, to propose marriage to her the moment I arrive back.

In the morning, as soon as I am dressed, I contact the hotel's travel desk.

"Urgent business requires that I leave for home without delay," I tell a woman in a cerise suit. "I must catch the next flight."

She examines my ticket and frowns.

"This ticket not exchangeable," she says apologetically.

"It doesn't matter," I say. "I'll pay whatever the difference is."

"It may be a lot," she says, tapping away at a computer.

I pay the difference — it is expensive, five months' rent — and though there is no flight until midnight, having made the reservation I am relieved of further culpability, return to my room, spend the day reading.

It seemed like forever before the sun began to set.

And then, two hours before I am scheduled to depart I leave the hotel, for what reason I am not quite sure, a return of curiosity, perhaps even a resurgence, I would have to admit, of some kind of desire. I make my way through the crowds to the famous street, find myself at an outdoor bar, next to a man who believes somehow that it is his right to insert his fingers into a strange girl's body, in full view of the world, inches from the nose of the straight-laced and immaculately conceived Buber. It is appalling but I am transfixed. As I watch, a girl approaches me. She is infinitely desirable, all skin and hair and imploring smile.

She places her hand on my leg.

"What your name?" she says. "Where you stay?"

I hear a man behind me, a German by the sound of it, discussing his visit to a venereal disease clinic. "My knob's getting as gnarled as a tree trunk," he declares with pride, and to laughter.

I hand the girl some money, smile at her disappointment, walk back onto the street and find myself at the entrance to a little alley I had not noticed before, now, unexpectedly, out of the rush. Before me are several establishments of one kind or another and one in particular catches my eye. Above the doorway is a sign "Star of Love Bar," and there are several girls in red robes sitting on stools at the door. They do not cajole the passersby, but sit instead talking among themselves. I stroll across to take a closer look and then find myself entering a long room, quite dark, with a bar counter to one side and a series of booths on the other.

Girls are seated about the room and one of them comes forward as I enter.

"Hello, welcome," she says, and several others join her, calling "welcome" from all corners of the room. "You like something?" she adds.

I tell her that I am just looking.

"Okay," she says simply and then, to my astonishment, she takes me by the crotch of my pants and leads me to a booth.

Let me describe the situation I am in. There are two Japanese men sitting at the bar, one of whom is smoking a cigarette as he gazes absently at the ceiling. This alone would not be out of the ordinary of course, except that kneeling on a pillow between his legs is a girl, and it is obvious that she is fellating him. There is no self-consciousness in it, not in the man whose face shows his pleasure, nor in his companion who sees no need to watch, makes a comment to him from time to time, drinks from a bottle of beer.

"You like?" the girl asks and I shake my head.

"No thank you," I say.

"You sure?"

"Very sure."

Her name is Pla, she says, and adds that it means fish, and when I ask her why this is so, why anyone would have named her "Fish," she says it is because of the shape of her mouth. Hearing this I do see something about her mouth

65

that would justify the name, not an under-bite exactly, but a broadness in the teeth so that when she laughs it is as if she is gaping for air, using her mouth as a fish might, though oddly, endearingly.

"My name is Alfred," I say, and she nods and repeats it. "Afled."

The bar is almost empty and other girls drift towards us and join Pla on the seat beside me. Each is unique, of course, but there is a sameness to them, a certain coarseness for all the tiny waists and slender hands, a nut brownness to their skin, a broadness of feet.

"Where you from?" one of them asks.

"The United States," I say. "Boston."

"One day I go there," she says, and as I look at her, her open red robe, her bobbed hair, I doubt it.

"How is America?" she asks.

I see, several booths away, a girl sitting at a table drinking a cup of tea, an open book in front of her. She looks up briefly and I see that she has dark lips, braided hair, eyes the color of clay. She is trying to decipher the book that lies open in front of her, struggling with something, it seems. Her brow furrows and then smooths, her lips move.

Something about her tugs at me.

"America is very cold now," I reply. "Snow everywhere. Ice on the ground. Very cold."

As I speak I look across at the dark girl sitting alone at the table. It is as if I have seen her face elsewhere, some-where cold, smothered in a down suit, a woolen hat pulled tightly about her ears.

"What's that one's name?" I ask, pointing to her. "What is she reading?"

"Nok," Pla says. "She new. Learn English."

I look at the girl again. She could be anywhere, in any classroom, struggling with her homework, diligently reading a novel. Of course she is not. It is an illusion, obviously, but there is something chaste about her, something studious. Whatever it is she is reading is covered in brown paper.

She sees me looking across at her, looks quickly down.

"You like her?" Pla asks.

"Yes," I say.

There ensues a heated discussion in this little bar and I listen, understanding nothing of it. It is a language filled with sour vowels and swallowed consonants, but whatever they have said the girl, Nok, stands up and straightens her red robe, closes the book, disappears into the back of the bar. When she emerges she is carrying a pillow and her little basket, the one with the cartoon sticker, the box of Kleenex, the mouthwash. I watch transfixed as she comes towards me, places her fingertips together in greeting, sets the pillow at my feet.

She stands for a moment, sedate, polite, bows her head as if she is about to seat me in a restaurant. I am surprised at how small she is, like a doll almost, draped in a robe. The lapels of her robe have been fingered, are, in places, soiled. She begins to kneel on the pillow.

"Wait," I say, and she looks up enquiringly. She is slight, though not insubstantial, not as insubstantial as the others have seemed, not a gathering of brown tendrils of no possible substance.

She waits, says nothing. There is a look of vague disappointment on her face as she waits. I suspect I am reading too much into it when I say that she looks ashamed. She is expected to tempt and she has not.

"No," I say after a moment. "Go ahead."

The girls stay where they are, chatter, watch with the sort of interest one would have if, for instance, Nok were changing a bandage on my leg. As she performs her task one girl strokes my arm, another my hair. Nok's actions are earnest, serious, pleasing. Her face, when I see it, when she looks up, is calm, unemotional. She smiles, tilts her head.

There is a Madonna video playing on the television and one of the girls asks if I like the music. I have fastened my clothes. Nok has disappeared into the back room presumably to clean herself. I am suddenly as weary as I have ever been.

"Yes," I say. "I like."

"I like too," she says, and then, without further preliminaries, she pulls me up from the bench and begins to dance with me and then we are dancing quite close together, her head on my shoulder, my arm around her waist. I close my eyes and suddenly I find myself overwhelmed by a sense of sadness and loss, thinking of Rhodesia and my father's old Morris car, of Henshaw and of my almost completed house, of Rebecca sprawled across my bed, of the great distances still to travel before I am home. I think of my hotel room with a suitcase lying opened on the bed, of white sheets, dark shining hair, polite nods, of the years of my life that are left, of my parents and their archaic beliefs, of their scarcely genteel poverty, of the poverty of these girls. For some inexplicable reason I sense that my eyes have filled with tears, that I am holding this girl far too tightly even as she says nothing in protest.

The music finishes and for a moment I do not release her and we stand together in the middle of the floor. As I take my arm from her waist she looks up at me and then touches my shoulder.

"American man okay?' she asks.

"Okay," I answer.

These people have seen everything, I am sure. A displaced and weepy foreigner cannot be the most unexpected event in the Star of Love Bar. I see that Nok has returned from the back room. She has put on her red robe, fastened it now in the front as if there is some newfound need for virtue, a place here for chastity.

She has roped her hair back, is rubbing cream onto her face with small flicks of her fingers.

"You okay?" she asks.

Her eyes are bright and earnest. She is carrying her book.

"What is that book?" I ask, and reach for it.

She offers it to me with both hands. It is the kind of booklet one might give a child to teach it its first few words. There is a picture of a bus and the word, "bus," a car, a toothbrush, a house.

"How good is your English?" I ask and she says: "Only a little."

"This isn't the best way to do it," I say. "There's got to be something better."

She shrugs.

"Friend give this me," she says.

I have noticed a bookstore nearby, stepped in earlier for a few moments of respite.

"I'll get you something better," I say, and Nok, as unsure what to make of the offer as I am of the reasons I am making it, says only, uncertainly, "Okay."

"Do you want to come with me?' I ask, and she says, "If I leave, you must pay the bar fine. Better I wait for you."

Mercy. Buber the educator scurries from the bar on his mission to spread Christianity to those who have recently orally serviced him. As the door closes I hear a heated discussion break out, shrill voices, can only guess at its content. I find the bookstore, its English as a Second Language section, flip through its selection. I don't know what I'm looking for. *ESL: Elementary Job Interview Skills.* Now what skills would those be for this time and place? I have a plane to catch, a taxi ordered, a blow job girl waiting for upliftment. I make my selection and walk back briskly.

As I approach, the girls on the stools outside the bar come to life. One of them leans over and presses the buzzer and the door opens. Inside I find that a group of men has arrived and is prospecting. One of them is talking to Nok, one hand on her shoulder, another on her stomach. He is stroking but also probing.

She stands quite still. I seethe.

"Nok?" I say.

She puts her hand on the man's arm, moves it away, asks him to excuse her.

"Many other girl," she says and then, pointing to me, adds, "my boyflen."

Oh does that show of loyalty not move the chemicals about. I hand her the book and she leads me to the back of the bar. There are several folding chairs and she sits on one, gestures for me to sit beside her. She goes through the book carefully, one page at a time.

"I think this one better," she says after a while. "I want . . . I wish . . . to English."

"To speak English," I correct.

"To speak English," she says.

"And to get a good job," I add. "A clean job."

"*Clean?*" she says with difficulty, and we flip together — she turns some pages, I others — to the back of the book. We find the word in the glossary.

"Oh," she says softly and then she looks back down. "Yes. A clean job."

I look at my watch, know that I have to leave. I reach for my wallet, open it, extract the remainder of my currency. She looks at the money, a lot by any measure, puts her hand on mine, presses it away.

"It okay," she says. "Not necessary."

I look across at her, at her upturned face, her slender hand on my arm.

"I'm sorry," I say, "for that," and gesture at my lap.

Her smile drops, her face clouds.

"No sorry," she says. "My job. Only job."

"You're lovely," I say, but it is clear she does not understand. She stands, looks at something in the room, at the row of liquor bottles against the wall, the television set with its karaoke tape.

"I could marry someone like you," I say on impulse, my hand going now from my heart to her breast.

She smiles, looks at me as if what I have suggested is not as preposterous as it obviously is, has no weight but is not entirely a joke.

"Okay," she says. "I wait you."

⸺

I stayed in Paris for two days but I saw little of the city. I remained mostly in my room, ate in none of the restaurants I had so carefully noted in my book, read instead from a guidebook so that I could, on my return, dissemble, describe places I was supposed to have visited as if I had, in fact, done so. I sampled instead a French McDonald's, an airport hotel cafeteria, sandwiches sold at a kiosk. On the morning I was to leave I walked around for an hour or two, lingered in the lobby of the Louvre, circled the Eiffel Tower, briefly entered Notre Dame. They all seemed very austere to me.

All along, surrounded there by the monuments and cathedrals, all I could think about was my behavior, that moment in the Star of Love Bar with shadows around me, the contemplative young woman reading a book in the bad light at the back of the bar and then responding, without any visible emotion, to my summons. She had a clear brown face, kind eyes, was an island of calm in a black sea, another displaced person, self-contained, observant. This is absurd, of course it is, but I felt as if there were something about her that I recognized, as if—and this is even more absurd—it was destiny, not a host of other things about which I knew nothing that had brought her to the moment in her life when I had found her.

At Orly airport I could have turned right around and gone back to set things right, but of course I did not. I dutifully boarded my flight, leaned back, tried to sleep as we cruised over the Atlantic, felt my heart sink as we approached the coast of Newfoundland and then came in over New England. During the last hour of the flight I felt that if I could not be off the plane and moving freely, waving my arms wildly in the air and breathing fresh air, I would burst. I remember pacing up and down the aisle cursing myself, my weakness, my vanity, my cupidity. Soon I would be home, sadder, poorer, not much wiser, but done with the notion of depraved excursions once and for all.

Or at least so I thought. I took a taxi straight to the rooming house, slipped into my room and without turning on the light tiptoed to my bed and slept for two days. When I finally awoke the whole thing seemed never to have happened.

I called Nigel to let him know I was back, and at Henshaw & Potter, when asked about Paris, I raved about its beauty.

"Don't we have something here, Alfie?" Rebecca asked several nights after my return. "You'd hardly have noticed the cost of the extra ticket, and it wouldn't have cost anything extra once we were there. You never think about my feelings."

"I don't see what you're upset about," I said. "It's not as if you and I were going together. And I say nothing when you bring other men to your room."

"But I always end up back here," she insisted. "There's a difference. I didn't used to think I could, but I could get into you, Alfie. Really I could."

I proudly present this snippet from the romantic diary of the great romantic Alfred Buber for the sole purpose of bringing my liaison with Rebecca to a close. My delusional dream about her aside, it was quite dead with her now. She would not let me make a break of any kind while we still lived under the same roof, and in the end I moved, several weeks before it was ready for me, into my uninhabitable house. The furnace had not yet been installed, though there was enough electricity to run a series of space heaters. Some things were finished and others quite rough, all manner of wires and fixtures hung haphazardly from the walls, but even so I pitched a tent in the living room and lived like a squatter, surprising the workmen each morning who would stumble across my campsite before going to work in a buzz of mumbled remarks and secret glances.

"Why did you move now?" Nigel asked. "You've waited so long and you tell me this house of yours is nearing completion. Why on earth would you move in before it is ready? Besides anything else it must be dangerous."

"There's no danger in it," I answered vaguely. "I needed to move now for all sorts of reasons. The rough living is temporary."

"So you've said," he observed dryly.

Take from this what you will. Compared to what I had seen, compared to Nok, Rebecca seemed, my relations with Rebecca had begun to seem, unspeakably vulgar.

The heart may be a lonely hunter. It is also an irrational demon.

CHAPTER FOUR

For a long time we resisted, at Henshaw & Potter, the temptation to which so many of the city's other firms have succumbed, to wear our success and longevity on our sleeves, so to speak, by means of highly opulent quarters and facilities that incorporate the most recent technological developments. As time passed I found myself more and more an advocate for leaving things as they were, for resisting the temptations so many people placed in our path to leap off into all sorts of uncharted directions. I became known, so I gathered, as something of an intransigent, a bulwark of the old ways. I did not support, for instance, the idea of allowing casual dress in the office, nor was I ever persuaded that computers enabled lawyers to work from home as easily as they could from our place of business. People must come to work, and they must be appropriately dressed when they do. That is simply my view. There are virtues in decorum, are there not, and in a punctual and consistent attendance at one's place of employment. What would be the purpose of rearguing matters that common sense suggests are either indefensible, or self-evident? *(I mean, what, in the end, is the purpose of a neck tie? One cannot defend it as rational, but the argument that one should simply discard it because of this suggests other ideas that do, in fact, verge on seditious. Or at least they do to me.)*

So I defended our systems against encroachment because I was unconvinced that what was being proposed to replace them were truly improvements, not merely innovations. It seemed to me that the two were often confused.

"I suppose," Henshaw was apt to say at the close of a discussion on some new expenditure or other, and not long after I became a partner and so free to speak my mind, "that we can count on our friend Buber for a 'nay.'"

There would be a chuckle or two. The innovation would fail.

I do not know anymore whether there is truly an inconsistency in this, the yawning chasm between my public presentation and my private thoughts and practices. It seems to me at times that they are not inconsistent, that one's insistence on a stiff and antiquated gentility can coexist without great irony with a personal life detached from any conventional mooring. That said, I readily admit that I lacked the courage to put this proposition to any sort of a test. It would have been over the alderman issue that a collision was most likely. There really was a faction in the town that felt quite passionately I should serve.

I found myself acting as a spokesman for ideas that made eminent good sense to me, but on which others of like mind were somehow tongue-tied. Just picture it, then, me standing in our waspish town hall sounding off on one parochial issue after another. Hear the loud applause when I am done.

"It is our job to civilize our children," I heard myself saying. "Civilized children are well-educated children, and to educate children there must be books for them to read, and for there to be books for them to read we must properly fund our library. There is nothing generous about this. It is a matter of self-interest for those of us who may some day age and become dependent on the judgment of those who are now young."

People smiled as they clapped. It only takes someone to argue the point, I suppose, and for whatever reason I did think these matters were self-evident. Children must read or they will become cretins. It is not a matter of choice.

After each meeting, then, a small group would gather about me, young people who shuttled their offspring in station wagons and subscribed to beliefs I am sure I would in large measure repudiate, and urged me, of all things, to galvanize them. They were unremittingly earnest, harassed by their domesticity, alluringly wholesome.

"You're the only one who can do it, Mr. Buber," they would say before they drove off to their homes, to their families, left me to meander back to my empty house with its shining walls. "The way you put things is always so balanced. People respect you."

What would they have said, these same people, had they discovered that the Buber they saw as their champion was, so stealthily, so imperceptibly, a wholly different Buber too.

⸺⸻⸺

I had thought as I boarded the aircraft that brought me home after that first fiasco in Asia that nothing would be quite the same again, that I had crossed a line that could not be uncrossed, that the experience, its nightmarish quality, would leave a mark on me. But as the months went by and nothing changed I reverted to my old habits, loathsome, unhealthy, compelled, but with this new feature: Thoughts of the girl did not abate, not at all, instead gathered strength until they were constant. I saw her, I sensed her, as she sat each evening at the end of the bar, quietly reading, always the same brown-colored book, was called from her silence at random, responded, returned when she was done. I knew nothing of her, nothing at all, and yet at the same time it seemed as if I knew of her everything a man needed to know of a woman.

So even as I settled back into my routines, felt in doing so the light that comes at the end of a startling dream, I knew that I would, in some manner or other, be drawn back, and that not only would I see her, but that I was destined to complete what I had started. I had no idea how this might happen but the point was that her odyssey, in some ways, validated my own and I became in some strange way happier than I had been for a long time. I was less perturbed by the dissembling, the odd juxtapositions. Things had a purpose, a new context. I cannot describe it better than to say that I was convinced that somewhere, elsewhere, I existed in a truer and better form. Even as I sounded off in the town hall, I would flash for just an instant to the girl and her basket a world away; and there was something in it that was uniquely mine, that was sad but not sordid, something that endowed *me* with a peculiar kind of autonomy, a refreshing new independence. Can a normal person understand how this is? Perhaps not. I felt a kinship with a girl whose real name I did not know, a girl whose life was in many respects both an inversion of my own and a reflection of it.

How do I put this without becoming ridiculous? Maybe I don't.

"Did you try that little restaurant I told you about?" Henshaw had asked.

"Of course," I had replied. "It was wonderful. Nouvelle cuisine, but not sparse."

"Exactly," Henshaw had agreed.

His wife had drawn a little diagram for me with instructions on how to get there, something I had studied on the flight from New York, tracing a little path across the guide book map so as to be able to explain what I had passed along the way. Henshaw, I should repeat, make clear, was a figure of awe for me then, a mentor, a role model, always kind, and yet I felt no compunction in brandishing my newfound perfidy.

"Grace will be thrilled you took her suggestion," he had said. "She'll take it as quite a compliment that you thought enough of her to take her advice."

My colleagues put their successes to use nurturing sturdy children and building the steadfast little marriages I saw about me and of which I was terribly envious. They would bring their children to the office on Father's Day and I would hear them discussing prep schools and colleges, paper routes, little league.

"Katie's been held back a year," I might hear someone say. "We're a little disappointed."

I would see the girl, this Katie, and I would think: *I would not know how to feel disappointment if she were mine. I would be thrilled simply by her breathing. I would pour the best of myself into her, spare no effort, would recreate the world so that her happiness and safety were at its center.* But these were idle dreams. My partners' wives, women with carefully waved hair, handsome outfits, jeweled hands, mill to either side of me. They would wonder at it, struggle to reconcile what they believe they know of me with what I know of myself. They would doubtless jump to all sorts of conclusions about all sorts of things if they knew even a smidgen of the truth.

"That's disgusting," I hear in my ear. "Horrible."

So I floated about, spinning my stories of wine-tastings in the Loire Valley, antiquity hunts, came almost to believe as I prattled on that there was a kernel of truth to it, that I had been in Paris, had spent time at the places I blabbed on about — and then I would catch myself, wonder at myself. Paris bores me, the stupid restaurants with their elaborate concoctions bore me, there is nothing there that does not bore me. And so I talked on, but all along I was thinking: *I have something I did not have before.*

(I need no one to tell me that this is not so. I need no one to come blasting into my little white room to describe my delusions. I need no one to tell me that in contemplating my return I was treading on ice beyond thin, rushing in where angels went beyond fearing to tread, tumbling down a slope without a catchment. I knew those things. I did not care.)

"You've quite taken to travel," Nigel noted when I mentioned to him that I may be going away again.

He had a tendency to express concern in a careful, circuitous manner.

"A change in scenery, I have discovered, can work marvels," I had replied lightheartedly. "One needs to be open to new experiences."

"Coming from you that sounds rather implausible," he had said.

Nigel is the one person, I believe, who suspected that things were not what I represented them to be.

———୨୨୧———

It has long been a habit of mine, on some evenings after dinner, to stroll into the village and to browse through the bookstore's new acquisitions. I eat in what my housekeeper has come to call the White Room, this small atrium with its marble floor and toneless furniture. She does not approve of the room at all, but then she approves of very little I have in my home. She would prefer, she has told me, wood, raging fires in the winter, woolen fabrics, colored walls.

"This is not a house for living in," she has said more than once.

As the housekeeper clears the table I close my book, leave the house and walk between the elm trees down the driveway. They are fully grown now, tall and beautiful. Rescuing them from Dutch elm disease has been costly and complicated, but they are irreplaceable and it has been worth it. The wind is brisk, blows about the garden and lifts all manner of fragrance into the air. I pause at the gates and look back at the house, at the little gazebo shining there like a lantern on its man-made mound. It all resembles a silent carnival, a shower of light and glass, white pillars, faintly colored shadows. It does give me joy; it does, if only in silent seconds such as this.

I close the gates behind me, cut across a meadow, and intersect a small lane that leads to the main street. I like to approach the town from this angle. I come upon it from out of the shadows at the hardware store, and it is as if I have entered a theater set from somewhere in the wings. This is my home town, after all, this village, a stolid little place with its gaslights, cobbled sidewalks, carefully designed storefronts. Its preoccupations are small ones, trivial even by some measures. The fight over funding for the library, for instance, has been going on, or so it would seem, for a generation, manages to preoccupy people as a war might elsewhere, famine, a lack of rain. There is a reference to it in every conversation, it has divided neighbors, it has become shorthand for so much else, an entire approach to life—or so one would be led to believe. In the Rhodesia of my youth, it does seem that the adults worried equally over events rather more momentous, but who am I to say?

The bookstore is a messy, informal place and the owner a nodding acquaintance. I worry about her sometimes, how she can make a living in our small town with a store such as this with its dusty inventory and sloping shelves. Sometimes I have found myself on the verge of offering her advice, free legal advice from the mouth of the great savior Buber, but she has managed to survive without it, seems perfectly content.

What is her secret, I sometimes wonder? How can she not worry?

I find myself browsing along the shelves, looking about to see who else has entered, and then when I am satisfied that there is nothing to see in that regard, no new opportunities this night that might distinguish it from a thousand others—a thousand thousand others—I gravitate to the travel section to see what new books she has acquired with descriptions of the place that has acquired this space in my thoughts, but to which no one knows I have any ties. When I hear her steps on the wooden boards coming back to see how I am doing, I shut the book quickly and return it to its shelf.

And what might she say that would be so terrifying?

"You're interested in Asia, are you, Mr. Buber?" she might observe.

"Somewhat," I would have to answer, and I would point casually at a picture of a temple standing somewhere on a hill, a golden Buddha.

"Well, you should go then," she would suggest. "I'm sure it's wonderful over there."

(Should I tell her that the place is hellish hot, burningly hot, with air filled by smoke and a cascade of fumes that defy parsing: exhaust, spice, cooking oil, chemicals? Should I tell her that as I stand there looking at her pictures I see images that would shock her to her shoes? Should I tell her about Nok?

Only to the impure are all thoughts impure.)

But it is not, after all, Asia that she wishes to talk about.

"Mr. Buber," she says instead. "I do wish you'd reconsider your answer about running for the board of aldermen. The candidate who purports to think the way we do—and you know who I mean—is running for all the wrong reasons."

"I can't," I say, "though I appreciate your confidence."

"We'd work so hard to support you," she says. "Are you quite sure?"

"Quite sure," I say.

Before the days of Nok—now everything is different. Everything is impossible, beyond comprehension—I used to consider how a decision to do so might bring to light some of my proclivities, make me answerable in a new way.

"Is it true, sir, these rumors? What is it, exactly, that has occurred?"

I sometimes think that one's self-respect is unrelated to how others regard one, and sometimes that how others regard one is all there is to self-respect.

⸻

There comes a time, after walks through the garden, explanations of how things work, the lovemaking too, that we must venture out, Nok and I, beyond the wrought-iron gates and into the little town with its colonial storefronts and ever helpful attendants. I touch a button under the dash and the gates swing open, turn my car onto the country road, and pass through my own village, and the next, head for a town some miles away.

I do not think she has anything but the vaguest notion of the curiosity she will provoke. Eyebrows will be raised, though this may well be imperceptible to all but me. People will be polite. Unnervingly solicitous. We have discussed this, of course, we must have, Nok and I, before we dare to venture out so brazenly: the sensitive topic of her background, how we came to meet, what it is she is doing here. She has listened carefully. She has seemed to understand.

What I have constructed is plausible, ambiguous, and adequate.

The stores are beautiful, filled with Christmas decorations, colorful islands in a landscape of gray and white. We look in the windows, she listens as I explain the artifacts, and then she surprises me by asking for something, something whimsical, a stuffed animal, and I buy it for her.

The clerk watches us carefully, takes my money, and hands the animal over with a certain reserve.

"Your change," she says. (*"Semi-literate, so far as I can tell. And young enough to be his daughter."*)

She will want as well, Nok will, and before too long, food that is familiar to her. We may drive in my absurd, boat-like car with its tinted windows to an Asian restaurant in a town far away.

"Have many restaurant like this?" she asks, and I say that they do.

"I know to work restaurant," she says.

The implication may be that she can carry her weight, could get a job, or, more unsettling, that she would like to spend some time among her own kind. Either way I do not respond. She orders plate after plate and then picks at the edges, leaving half-eaten food scattered about the table so that it resembles nothing so much as the end of a hurried buffet. I don't know how she sees this, that it costs money, that to order and then leave behind is a wasteful thing to do, but I suspect that is not a part of her analysis. Endless bounty is part of the bargain I myself have not so implicitly suggested, no? Of course, we are a spectacle, not only among the other diners, but among the wait staff who stand against the walls and speak behind their hands, speculate, smile, in all likelihood see things for what they are.

On the way home she pays close attention to the stores we pass, and when she sees a similar restaurant less than a mile from the house she points it out and asks, quite reasonably, "Why we not go there?"

Why indeed?

How can she know that she is simply a figment of the imagination, that her legs, so smooth and childish and easily parted, are not only her own but those of a thousand others, that her beauty even is not hers, her charm how she can be made to step from oblivion and then be made to step back into it, how she can be conjured up and then discarded without explanation? How can she be brought to understand such things? It would be like trying to explain water to a fish, or a camel to an Eskimo.

But you have brought her home, you great messianic Buber, you and no one else. You have made the decision, the commitment. Now be a man even if it feels impossible, a dead end beyond dead ends, a daydream beyond reason.

I have no choice then, don't you see, but to try again. Time is passing, time has passed, a month and then two and then six, a year, and still the days roll by. Each day as I complete my time card, hand to my secretary the log of who will be billed for what, I have a sense that I am turning over the hours like rocks to see what lies beneath; and that each time it is nothing, that each day the wick is further burned and that soon my visit will be as irrelevant as events in Salisbury, as anything else that has faded to nothing. If I am to return, how much longer can I wait? Even there, even there where options are so few, time passes.

This time, though, the world traveler is off to Turkey.

"The Byzantine buildings in Istanbul are some of the most beautiful in Europe," he finds himself saying. "It's the point where everything Ottoman ran headlong into everything Catholic."

"Each to his own," Henshaw remarks. "You always did have eclectic interests, and I say: Pursue them."

"I can't wait to visit the Topkapi museum and the hot springs on the southern edge of the Black Sea."

What of her, in the meantime? How many men? I see her in her room counting her take, soiled banknotes folded into a plastic purse, these for this need, these for that, and

82

more tomorrow. Her red robe lies on the bed, in need of a wash. Her face is soft. Her lips are parched.

Who are her parents? What do they know of this? What are their concerns? What are their wishes and dreams for their lovely daughter? I must know these things, and the urgency in it has not degraded, not one bit over the wasted months. This curiosity is endless, this need to know more, to understand why it is that what I have seen feels—laugh if you will, bend over in scorn at the absurdity of it if you will—something like love.

"I wait you."

How about a Bubery vignette?

There is a youngish woman and her son sitting in the seats beside me on the final leg of the flight to Asia and I am annoyed at how little discipline she exercises. The lout is playing a computer game, his plastic board squeaking and jingling as if no other passenger should mind it. He looks unhygienic too in soiled jeans and with hair ostentatiously matted. I try to ignore him, but it is difficult.

I have brought with me a series of books of varying degrees of lightness—P. G. Wodehouse and Evelyn Waugh at one end of the spectrum, John Updike in the middle, Henry James at the other, all of which I have previously read and enjoyed—and for a while I sit reading about Rabbit Angstrom and his poor lost Janice as the afternoon turns rapidly into night, and the bells and buzzers beside me continue unabated. Rabbit leaves Janice, runs, and then within days he has Ruth, a choice to make. It is the kind of choice I don't know much about, one kind of woman or another, to leave one, to want more.

I put the book away, lift the *Wall Street Journal* from a rack in the front of the craft.

"We had to read that for a whole semester," the lout says suddenly. "It was boring as shit. Do you read that because you want to or because you have to?"

"Nothing is interesting if you do it only because you have to," Buber intones.

"You better believe that," he answers and returns to his game.

"Tell me," Buber, engaged now, asks. "Didn't you find anything in here that you were curious about? And why must you curse simply to make a point?"

But he has left me, the boy, returned to his own pursuits. And I, I glance at him, his earphones, his eyes fixed on the machine in his lap. He is a handsome boy once one sees past the grime, and he is insolent and too casual, but there is something about his sloth that one senses will be easily unleashed into something else, something new and strong, when he chooses. He languishes in the certainty of it.

I sit snugly in my seat, a book on my lap. I envy him.

———

The must brings it back more vividly than could any daydream, a heaviness in the airport air that smacks of rattan counters and white linen suits, of anticipation and elation and the deepest of disappointments. I exit into the jangling night, into the wet air and towards the quarreling line of taxis. There is, in my step, nothing furtive, an overlay of purpose. Perhaps I am emboldened by the very absurdity of it, the absurdity of my quest, that I should have come back on so flimsy a pretext having scurried away so ignominiously before.

There is the matter of choosing a driver, of slinging a bag into the trunk, of giving directions. The driver turns the key, the engine sputters, and we head out into the traffic. In the window I see myself, familiar face, shining pate, day old growth.

"How long you here?" the driver asks.

For some time he has been eyeing his prospect in the rearview mirror.

"A week," I say. "Maybe more."

"You been here before?" he asks, and I say, "Many, many times."

I open the window and let in the choking air.

"You like girl?" he asks.

"No thank you," I say.

"Nice girl," he insists.

I don't reply, adopt a faintly disapproving posture.

We speed by the haphazard skyscrapers, the night markets, the roadside stalls, the staggering temples with their impossible trimmings and garlands and golden tiers. Spirals of smoke flail from a thousand exhausts. At the reception desk immaculately groomed hostesses in lilac outfits see me through the paperwork, cash my money. From somewhere in the distance comes the throb of disco music, a shout, engines roaring. The air, even inside, smells faintly of petroleum fumes, outdoor barbecues, incense. This is not where my bones, where the cells in my body, are meant to be.

I am decanted into a room with elaborately patterned fabrics, moldy air, a television, little packages of soap. The door finally closes, I open my suitcase, extract from it only what is absolutely necessary, undress, shower, shave, ride the elevator back to the lobby. It all happens very quickly. It is all faintly comical. The heat is oppressive. In Boston, where they think I am in Turkey, it is midday yesterday. The hotel receptionists watch me with a knowing passivity, offer nothing beyond hands clasped in greeting, a wall of smiles. I am propelled from the hotel by a revolving door, too abruptly from the coolness of the lobby and into the night. All about is this great commotion, moving cars, chugging samlors, motorcycle engines, unbreathable air. It is midnight, but one would scarcely know it from the coming and going, the beery men with sylphy girls on their arms, the noises, jubilant, carefree, loud.

Outside I run the gauntlet of taxi men and touts and move off in the direction of the Star of Love Bar. The street is thick with people laughing and pointing and weaving among the stalls, with girls, bendy brown forms in short dresses, legs and arms and long dark hair, with water and garbage and neon lights and engines. I look down at my suede Cole Haan loafers, my pants made of cashmere—cashmere here, on this cacophonous Hades of a sidewalk; yes, but so finely woven, so porous, breathing, cool—and marvel at it all. In the fragrant store on Newbury Street they know me, trot out their best and most costly, stand admiringly against the wall as their portly little Micawber struts around in clothes designed for the taller and better. The shoes are nice. They are part of the Buber as he lives in that other world, carried onto this disconnected stage on stubby-toed little feet, vapors of sweat filling them now as they tread on the gumstained sidewalk, step over muddy puddles, walk beside a narrow canal in which floats who knows what, cabbage leaves, a dead rodent, other unmentionables.

I search out the odiferous little terrace with its flagstones and clammy chairs, but things are not quite as I have remembered them. What then leads me to believe that boredom, illness, some petty dispute, some change of heart, will not have caused her too to disappear without a trace? Or worse yet. What if I find her not in the back of the bar where I have imagined her, back where it is quiet and dark, with a book, but on her knees crouched before some filthy man?

"Can you direct me to the Star of Love Bar?' I ask a policeman.

He gives me a bemused and unsympathetic look.

"Many places to drink," he says, gesturing.

"I show you," a teenage boy beside him says.

I walk behind him for a block or two and then realize he is trying to steer me into several places of his choosing. I peel away and he tries to pursue me.

"What your problem, man?" he shouts and then, as an afterthought adds, "You want Rolex?"

He pronounces it *Lolex*.

It is surely folly to yearn too deeply in a place such as this.

———— ✾ ————

I keep picturing her—get this—in a down jacket, ski tips pointed ahead, sitting beside me on a lift somewhere, sliding slowly into the mountains. The world below us is white and clean, will look like a postcard to her, like nothing she has seen before. The wind will wind about us, touch the napes of our necks, blow dustings of snow across the mountain edge below. She will stand unsteadily at the peak and I, dressed too in a down suit, goggles, knitted cap, will stand beside her and take her arm, and then we will begin our careful descent.

I can hear nothing but the silence, see nobody but ourselves.

***

In the end it is not that difficult, the world-famous street is not that long that it can conceal forever the Star of Love Bar with its smeared patio and dirty windows, its crooked neon sign with the outline of a slender figure, fingers at her lips. Several girls in their red robes are draped over stools at the door. They look bored, eat from a common bowl, talk, gesture. From time to time one or the other of them will gesture to a passerby, beckon in raucous terms. One of them crouches with a leg tucked under, exposing her thigh, slender and brown, both vulgar and appealing.

I approach slowly and examine each of their faces. They are not familiar.

One of them notices me.

"Mister," she shouts. "Come in, mister."

I watch her, her expression exuberant, eager, mocking. She will be surprised when I do not ignore her, when I accept. She is older than many of the girls who flit about here, perhaps in her thirties. Her face has an edge of cynicism, is worn. Other men, I see perusing, walk by.

"Yes, yes," she says as it becomes clear that I am, in fact, a customer. "Welcome."

They are eating from a large bowl of rice, taking little wads and dipping them in an orange-colored sauce. Their meal is fragrant. As I reach the door she presses a button and I sense a quick stirring in the darkness within.

"Hello sir," comes the chorus. "Welcome."

The bar looks exactly as I have remembered it. There is a counter on one side, chairs pressed up against it, several crescent-shaped couches along the wall. A pornographic movie shows on the television set. There are two men sitting on barstools, and between the knees of each of them I see glimpses of red, of red fabric, rocking. One of the men reaches across and takes a bottle from the counter.

They crowd around me, the girls, they crowd me, chattering, flattering, solicitous. A hand is on my shoulder, another touches my trousers even as I edge my way inside.

"You like?" I hear.

"Is Nok here?" I ask. "Nok?"

My question sets off a flurry of discussion, head shaking, pointing.

"Nok not here," one of the girls says. "Nok gone. Choose another girl."

I am guided to one of the crescent-shaped couches and sit, am offered a drink, try to adjust to the dimness of the lighting. The place is the same, but not a single face, not one, is familiar. The street is built on shifting sands, this I know, but I have not expected them to shift so entirely in the space of a few months. As I sit girls descend on me and position themselves on either side like butterflies settling on a cactus.

The older woman, the one who first spoke to me, kneels at my feet. She looks up with an expression that for a moment is clear of suggestion, but then she licks her lips lewdly and I shake off my torpor.

What a mistake I am in the process of making. What a mistake.

"No thank you," I say.

She reaches up nevertheless and places her palm on my trousers. The air smells of beer, of smoke, faintly of antiseptic. I reach down and remove her hand but she is no novice, knows when she has elicited her response.

What a catalog of mistakes. I am tired, stiff, old.

"Is Pla here?" I ask.

Now I *have* elicited a response, a flurry of discussion, great animation. Shall I read meaning into a dialog of which I understand not a word? The elder at my feet is indignant. Let things be, she shouts, her hand waving, and sooner or later I will knead my way, stroke my way to acquiescence, to the point of no return.

No, others say, heads shaking. What is Pla's is Pla's.

"Do you know Pla?" I ask and then, on a whim, I make a fish mouth of my own just to convince her of my legitimacy, to let her know that this is not a whim, that I know this Pla, this fish mouth girl, and that I will be tenacious.

"I know," someone says, and this sets off another round of chatter, indignation from the woman at my feet who stands, closes her robe, storms out of the bar.

"What's the problem?" I ask and a girl beside me says, sweetly, convincingly, "She like you."

One of the men at the bar turns around and smiles, shakes his head, returns his attention to the red robe at his lap.

"Where is Pla?" I ask.

"Pla not here," my new ally says. "She come tomorrow."

"Does she still work here?" I ask.

"Yes. She with customer."

"Oh," I say.

"I come with you now," the girl says. "Tomorrow, I bring you here, you find Pla."

Oh Buber, you bleary-eyed old fool, drained of desire, empty, homesick for a sterile room half a world away. I am one thing to these people—I know this—one thing only, and beyond that there is no one on this earth who can place in context the rotund little fellow on the couch, no one who would care to. Perhaps there is no other context. Perhaps it is true that it does not matter, that nothing matters.

I am weary from the hours of travel, the time change, the commotion about me. One could sit back, one could, one could close one's eyes and sink into the meat of it, the thick air of it, the nothingness of it. Nothing matters. We all die. Beautiful thighs and riches and paintings and elegant homes do not matter.

"What time will Pla be here, do you think?"

I must—indulge me—come up for air. I know, you see, how it all ends, who does and doesn't lie sprawled across my bed, who sat on a sweaty train for hours on end as it snaked through the countryside, past rice paddies, green and muddy and dotted with buffalos and stick people in frayed clothing, through stations where vendors pass the windows to offer fried grasshoppers and salted squid that resemble strips of starched canvas, along mountain ledges that drop away with terrifying suddenness. I know how it is to stand at a fork in the path and to sense that either course holds its own whiff of shame.

My home, my beautiful home. There is nobody who is awake now but me. I open the gazebo door and walk out to the lawn. That bed there, the far one, needs weeding. Actually, there are things all about that could use attention. To my surprise I have allowed, even come to welcome, a certain derelict look in my mausoleum. I like the way the grass has gone a bit wild at the edges, the craggy look in what were once pristine flowerbeds. I like the feeling in the air that things have been allowed to go to seed.

The gardener, once a fixture, comes only every few weeks now at my request. He arrives, sighs, tackles only the most urgent of projects, heaves and hauls rather than trims and touches.

I know, you see, where Pla led me, what happened, what has followed.

———oooo———

A return to the Star of Love Bar, in daylight now. By day the famous road is a dirty mix of wet scraps and wrappers, of metal boxes and padlocked doors, scooters, wagons selling food, people. There are office workers in prim uniforms, men in suits. Sunlight dries some things out, exposes the wetness of others.

Again then the stools, the distracted girls in their red robes. They cast me a half-hearted kind of scrutiny and then a face or two comes alive in recognition.

"Hello handsome man," one of them says. "Your girl-friend inside."

I take the mockery for what it is.

"Handsome," I say. "I think not."

"Handsome, true," the girl insists, and she makes a gesture over her face, outlines, who can mistake it, a large round nose.

As I pass she reaches out and grabs my leg, pulls me toward her.

"Flat nose no good," she says.

I feel her hands traveling about me, work myself free.

"Is Pla inside?"

She leans over and pushes the door open a few inches. An odor of antiseptic seeps from the dark room. I catch a glimpse of a girl on a barstool resting her head on her folded arms. She appears to be asleep.

"Pla!" the woman shouts, and lets go of the door.

The door slams closed like a gunshot, but I hear movement behind it. Pla emerges into the street, pulls her robe about her, looks at me without even a glimmer of recognition.

"Pla," I say. "I remember you."

"Yes?" she says.

She looks me over with curiosity. She is in her twenties, perhaps, ruffled. It is too early in the day, her manner suggests, for any intrusive demands.

"Yes?" she repeats.

Oh, I will spare us all the pidgin exchange, the explaining, the incredulity. I will skip right over it because it is obvious what has to be said, what I want. Picture this, though: Buber standing at the bar peeling off banknotes as he pays the bar fine that will free this Pla to spend a week accompanying him to that place of pilgrimage, the Village of Nok. The bartender is impassive as he gestures for more and more, and Buber keeps peeling, peeling away at the Henshaw & Potter dollars until finally he is informed that the spigot may close.

To his left a series of grunts, like a pig dying. A brown arm closes a zipper, disengages, a girl disappears into the dark reach of the bar where Pla is already changing from her red robe into blue jeans, a tee shirt, and scuffed white shoes with heels of treacherous thinness.

—∞∞—

Come on the journey, please. It is of a kind you are not likely to take yourself. It is of a kind I am not likely to have taken. One man's fool's errand is another's National Geographic extravaganza.

Don't mention it.

"Is there no way to telephone her?" I have asked. "No shop or hotel nearby that we can call and pay to send for her?"

"No," Pla insists. "Farmer only."

She meets me at the station with a backpack and two large boxes she can scarcely lift—there are the oddest things inside, I see later, canned fruit, computer games, more shoes than she can possibly need—and she negotiates us through the various stages of our departure. I hand her bills and she buys tickets, finds the right platform, and leads me to our carriage. As we walk past a line of vendors selling fruit and drink and cooking in all manner of pans at the edge of the platform, she suggests I take advantage of them.

"Is there a place to buy food on the train?" I ask her.

"This better," she says.

There is more to Pla, and far less too, than I have imagined. She is firm when she bargains, committed in her opinions as to where we should wait and when we should board, brooks no nonsense from the porters who try to carry her boxes. She is, when dealing with others, quite shrill, insistent, hard-edged. But she assumes also that because I have paid for her to leave the bar and arranged for her to come with me, I have bought her too.

She sits, as we wait to board, with her hand high on my thigh.

"Pla," I have already said, taking her by the shoulders, "I am going to see Nok. I want to see Nok. I don't want to have sex with you. I want you to show me where she is, and then nothing."

"No problem," she has said, and then she makes a lewd gesture with her tongue and lips as if I have just entered the Star of Love Bar and am wondering what is on offer. She does it out of habit, I expect, does it because she thinks every man wants it and that it is something I want too, whether I will acknowledge it or not.

It is also, I discover to my disappointment, about all there is of her that is accessible to me.

———

We find seats in a long coach, already quite full and with its aisles crammed with boxes, cases, a bicycle with its wheels removed and bound with rope as if it has been subdued with difficulty. There is air-conditioning because occasionally a cool little gust reaches my face, but it is easily overwhelmed. The crowd presses in, inquisitive, urgent. I remember a wistful fantasy of my father's as he extolled the virtues of Mao, "the masses of Asia," about which he once raved, that new breed of man on the precipice of achieving his socialist dream. This was before Vietnam, of course, before so many things, before the insistent, giggling faces that make me wince at his naïveté.

I have a map, know where we are going, though Pla has made clear that I will not find Nok's village on any map.

"Small," she says.

"Why did she go back?" I ask. "What was waiting for her there?"

"She miss her mother," my guide tells me. "Same many girls. Not happy in city."

"Did she know before she came what she would be doing in the city?' I ask, and Pla looks at me as if my question is almost unfathomable.

"Everybody know," she says.

I find myself, the only westerner in this coach, an object of unremitting curiosity. People take turns to approach me, to say a few words, to retire on exhausting their *repertoire*.

Small children point and laugh, one of them runs his fingers over the hair on my arm. The place is awash in speculation.

"Where are you going to, sir?" I am asked, and when I mangle the name of the village, Pla explains and a long dialog I do not understand, accompanied by much head nodding and pointed gazing, ensues. I am the center of attention and would rather not be, but what can it matter?

Dear Nigel, I could write. *Today I finally visited the Topkapi museum.*

Where did I get this capacity to lie? Who knows? And what will be the consequence of it? When will the axe fall, the other shoe drop?

I have lived too long to believe that this sort of deceit can occur without consequence.

It is early morning when we arrive at our destination. We have been traveling for over twenty-four hours; and as I step from the crowded train I am met by a new set of misgivings as I look about and see that we have come aground amidst not much of anything. The train has simply stopped at a sign beside a hut with a grass roof and no one in it, at a place known perhaps to the conductor, but without any obvious significance.

"This is it?" I ask Pla.

"Yes," she says. "Village that way."

She does not, as I look over at her, inspire confidence. I have had dreams where I have been marooned, unable to return to my point of departure, in a frenzy of uncertainty as to what I am expected to do. I feel a shadow of this now, out in a field who-knows-where with not a soul on this planet aware of where I am, not a soul on this planet other than this slight and raucous girl between me and every manner of possible mishap. I could sink into the mud here, disappear in the water of the rice paddy, and no one would know, not for a hundred years. I am unshaven, groggy, more than a little disoriented. I would deserve it.

The air smells lush, of mud and grass and animals. Pla looks especially small here in the country, teetering about the packed mud in her high heels.

"How far is it?" I ask.

"Not far," she says, but even to the edge of the horizon — and there is nothing but fields and trees between here and the horizon — is far.

"How far?' I ask.

She does not reply but, to my surprise, settles down in the shade and opens one of her boxes. She takes out a bottle of soda, unwraps a package, and offers me something to eat. I do not recognize what it is she is eating.

"Please tell me what we're supposed to do next," I ask.

—⚬⚬⚬—

Enough. Let me skip instead to the house in which Nok lives with her family. It is on stilts — would you believe it — ten feet or more above the ground, and whatever is not used, not needed, old water, for instance, discarded leaves, is simply heaved off the edge as if the whole world below were a receptacle, a giant garbage can. The wind blows it about, the sun bakes it, the rains come and wash it into gullies. Life is lived, all life takes place, on a wooden platform with floorboards that are old and weathered, but that do not mask the years of spilled food, the accidents of babies, a million million beads of sweat. Here I find myself, leaning up against a post, my little bag against a wall long since opened by a child. My changes of clothes, my razor, my toothbrush, what else, have been extracted, held up, played with, commented on.

Pla has attempted an explanation, said who knows what to an audience of dozens, to a crowd of uncles and aunts and neighbors and the curious, while I have sat like a statuette understanding nothing, fielding looks, skeptical nods, shaken heads. It is a pantomime out of Kafka, a trial, a cascade of *non sequiturs*. Has the Star of Love been mentioned, the little stools described, the clammy fabric of the curving couches, the soiled red robes? Who can say, but it goes on

95

and on. The sides of the platform on which we are conducting our proceedings are open to the elements. A man rises and saunters away from the group. He pauses behind a flimsy, waist-high weaving. He urinates onto the ground below.

Oh savior of the proletariat, Lady of Golders Green, what is the source of the impulse, where is the start of the trajectory, that leads from the manicured fields of Southern Rhodesia to this? Who are these people clacking away with their broken brown teeth, their feet as hard as buffalo hooves, and what have they to do with me? I sit on the crooked teak platform and I cannot be sitting here, cannot; it is impossible that I have brought about this ridiculous collision of lives and images and expectations, this juxtaposition so immense that it cannot be happening even as I steal glances at the young woman whom I have placed at the center of this hubbub, the soft and perfect product of these cawing peasants. She is perhaps the most beautiful young woman I have ever seen, demure against all odds, a pawn in this raging debate.

In the distance are sights of the most extreme exoticism, clumps of swaying coconut trees, fields of green so rich they defy description, ponderous plough animals, conical hats, clouds of gold. At some point she has risen, left, returned holding the cheap notebook I chose for her in the city a thousand years ago.

Buber sits in a dream, in a cloud all his own.

<hr />

It is the father, a deeply lined, wiry, unpleasant-looking man, with whom I need to contend. On arrival, sitting like Tom Sawyer or some wandering minstrel on the back of an ox-drawn cart (picture it: legs hanging from the back as the cart bumps over the rudest of lanes, dust caking cashmere socks, coating the tassels of expensive shoes), we are greeted by small children who ask excited questions and then disappear over a rise. The full delegation waits beneath the hut's stilts as we jangle into view. Tom Sawyer's legs swing about as the cart hits a bump, brush against Pla's stiletto heels.

(You will perhaps wonder at this, my dearest, how eager I am to share this, to remove from the concealed heart of Asia a scene of such ridiculousness. Perhaps a different man would leave it with the palm trees and the mud-soaked canals; but in light of all that came later – the harshness of the scandal – this begins to seem benign indeed, recalling it akin to building a firewall to protect against an approaching inferno. So I embrace the scene, take it in: Tevye Buber, ridiculous in his cashmere trousers, rocked about with dung and hay on the back of a wood-wheeled cart.)

There is furious dialog of course, more people are summoned. One would have thought this was a private matter, not the subject of a village convocation. One would have thought this was something to be discussed by Nok and me, not negotiated by Pla and Nok's father, nasty piece of work that he seems to be.

"Don't you value your daughter?" I long to ask. "Isn't the decent thing to tell this preposterous man, this caricature, to get lost?"

The excited voices, the pitch of it all, are not consistent with the invitation, the insistent gestures towards a shaky little stairway, a house on stilts. Nok lurks in the background, is somehow out of bounds.

"I'd like to speak to Nok," I say to Pla. "Alone."

"Cannot," Pla says. "In the city maybe. Here Nok belongs to father."

Be alert, you fool. How could you have missed what was coming?

⸺⸻⸺

They have not been offended that this big ugly blob of a foreigner would dare to desire their lovely young daughter. They have not been surprised that this big crass farting foreigner sitting like a clumsy ox against the pole has the audacity even to fantasize about placing his fat paws on their girl half his age. The debate has been, or so I learn, about money, about terms, about nothing else. They have

97

missed my mission, or Pla has misrepresented my mission, and though the full implication of this descends on me only slowly, at the end of it all I will be responsible for her, her guardian, by implication theirs too.

I am not, to them, or so it would seem, a blundering and deluded imposter at all. Their daughter is not, to them, a demure and desirable young woman, at all. There is a different balance to it, one I grasp only at the edge, lose, grasp again. A deal, it seems, and without a word from me, without any participation by Nok, is on the table.

"You have five hundred dollars?" Pla asks.

"What for?" I ask.

"You pay, you take Nok."

"Now look here," he says, blustering, ineffective, a little Englishy creep out of his depth. "What have you been saying to them? I didn't come here to *buy* Nok. I came to *see* her."

"Same thing," Pla says.

"It's not the same thing," I say. "You know that."

"Same same," Pla insists. "You pay now, after that, all up to you. Do what you want."

Oh for heaven's sake.

The upshot?

What else could it be? Buber's clumsiness will drive her from the safety of this dirty platform back to the greasy floor of the Star of Love Bar.

———

Well, there's more before we get to that.

How do you eat, you could ask, perched in the middle of nowhere with nothing familiar, no frame of reference, here in the world of the buffalo and the hut where Alexander Graham Bell and Thomas Edison and Louis Pasteur and Alexander Fleming are but the vaguest of abstractions? ("Do you have a moon where you come from?" someone will ask me, through Pla, pointing up at a zeppelin-sized apparition floating right above us.)

(*Oh, you snort, he deserves what's coming, if not for his smorgasbord of indiscretions, his absurdity, his roundness, and his vulgarity, then for his condescension. I agree. Look about, please. Now what else should I surrender?)*

From nowhere, it seems, a collection of bicycles, carts, even a motorbike or two, materializes.

"We go eat now," Pla says.

"Where?" I ask.

"Restaurant," she says.

This I cannot quite picture. Where would we find a restaurant?

"Good restaurant," she says. "I know this one."

I lose myself in a surge of movement, people going down the rickety stairs, down a rope ladder, others who have not been on the platform walking towards us as if summoned. Nok is sent, so it seems, on one errand after another, is ordered about by her father, by an elderly lady, by an older, quite overweight woman who I have been led to understand is her sister.

"She sit with you at dinner," Pla says, conspiratorial, clutching my arm.

I am given the place of honor on the pillion of one smoking motorbike, her father on another. Nok rides with her sister in a cart filled with relatives and neighbors. We arrive at our destination after a grinding ride well ahead of the others. There is, it seems, some sort of restaurant after all, an outdoor affair illuminated with colored lights strung about poles, decorated with national flags and old calendars pinned to walls, powered by a generator I hear throbbing faintly in the distance. The smells of food mix with those from the field. It is a heady mix.

Nok arrives in her cart and is now more or less pushed to my side. We are led to the head of the table, she and I, and it feels almost as if we are at a wedding feast, but there is no stopping it. In Salisbury they would lift Nok and me on our chairs, dance and sway and carry us about the room, but now we sit side by side, watch the merriment of the others. What has happened is far from clear to me, though five hundred dollars has now indeed changed hands.

Under the table I take Nok's hand.

Let me do something I am no good at, or rather something at which I have no practice. Let me be—let me try to be—poetic, to fasten onto what it is that has held me and allowed this all to progress unchecked.

There is the matter of that simple gold earring and the wisps of hair that break loose and feather over it, a forehead that is smooth and broad and eyelids lightly dusted with blue, there are the eyes that flit briefly down and then return one's look with radiance. There are teeth that are white and straight—this despite all manner of neglect—there are the delicate and subtle hands. There is more, ineffable things, grace amidst all this, the same grace as in the Star of Love Bar, distance, sadness, a quiet acceptance.

This too.

I am told, unceremoniously and after copious amounts of beer have been drunk, food ordered, it seems, for an entire neighborhood—much of which lies uneaten and will be wasted—that I am expected to pay for it; and of course, in line with everything else, this wave of sludge on which I am riding, I do, and with perfect passivity. In the back of a cart on the way home, though, Nok slips money into my pocket, returns to me from whatever pittance it is she has saved much of what I have just spent.

How can a gesture like that, under all of these circumstances, not move a man?

⸺⸺

I have seen on late night television, and more than a few times, a particular documentary which rivets me. It concerns an anthropologist who goes to some remote place in South America or the Philippines and finds a tribe almost untouched by modernity. You see pictures of him in his khakis, crouching among tribesmen barely clad, and then of him with a particular female, young and strong-looking, but oh so rough, enough footage of the background kind that even before it becomes explicit you begin to wonder, and rightly so. You learn that he marries this woman, and then you see her, uncomfortable in a parka, walking through a shopping mall in Seattle, and then children; and then you learn that she does, in the end, leave him and return to her village. He seems quite bereft by it, but having watched it unfold you can only say, you are compelled to say: What on earth else did he expect?

They sleep, in this primitive village, in some sort of communal room, also on a platform, perched, so to speak, up in the trees. I will sleep, I am told, on a roll against a reed wall with others all about me. I will wash from a giant trough, out in the open, cover myself with a sheet while doing so. I will do this because I have stepped off the track of my life by something irresistible but taking the shape of a girl.

There is, in her face, in her eyes, every dream I have ever had.

Oh it is not love, I know that. It is much more compelling. I do not know where it will lead and yet, and yet, it will lead where it leads. I am a man. She is a woman. Someday we will both be dead.

The chorus of the aghast be damned.

It is very late at night, or early in the morning, that I feel the first touches of what I know instantly will be debilitating illness. I have eaten with a measure of apprehension—who knows where all this has been prepared, who knows with what water and with what level of hygiene? But I have gone along, gone along, gone along, and now the price of this laxity begins to be felt, first in a generalized achiness, then in a fine layer of sweat that coats me within my sleeping roll, then in the onset of pains in my stomach.

I rise and the spasms intensify. I know I will not make it down the broken stairs. I am aware how distant any medical care will be. I feel as if I am about to die, simply to lose touch with the night and the air here in the middle of a field, and that it is a consequence richly deserved.

101

I sit instead on the top stair and hold my head in my hands. There is a great deal of snoring about, a rustling in the trees, the whir of crickets. If I pass out I will tumble to the ground, but I must get down, out into the bushes, away from these people. My stomach is foul, my throat is full, there is an avalanche of debris inside me.

"Nigel," I mutter. "You do not deserve to be dragged into this."

Fabric appears beside me and a hand rests on my shoulder. Nok guides me down the stairs and out into the grass.

———

It is possible, I suppose, that I could have died. To this day I have no idea what hit me, what it was that sent me so abruptly into what I later learned was a week of fever and delirium. I was adamant, they told me, that help not be sent for, that I stay where I was, that the thing resolve on its own, one way or another, and that this was what I desired.

It does not surprise me that through the fog of it all this was my only demand. I seem to remember something of it, how urgent it was that I not be moved into the open and that nobody from elsewhere be brought in to bear witness. They gave me local remedies, I am told, a mix of herbs and poultices and drops of broth when I would take them. Whether they helped or hindered the process I could not say.

Through it all Nok, my wife of sorts, remained a fixture at my bedside. I do remember her hands, the bracelets that tinkled at her wrists, cold cloths, a steady spoon, a gentle kneading at my temples. I remember a fragrance, a hand on my forehead, hair tracing a path across my chest as she leaned over me to straighten a sheet.

I remember something too of the delirium, but there were no great revelations in it. I know that I called for the lady from Golders Green more than once, conflated the places of my past and my present so that I was both back in Boston and in Salisbury, subject to the whims of my teachers and my law partners, sitting on a truck with my loafers dangling in the dust, and reversing my car from a garage though I had no ability to make it move. I mumbled about the Star of Love Bar, Nok has said — something of which those around us had their suspicions but no concrete knowledge — seem to remember constant motion, peoples' faces staring down at me, making suggestions, moving me. I remember being lifted as the mat beneath me was changed, the relentless heat, the thick, unbreathable air.

At some point my fever broke, and whatever it was I had ingested that had knocked me over so thoroughly began to clear of its own accord. I had overshot by a day or two the time of my scheduled departure. My concern — my panic — was that someone would notice and try to find me. Nigel could be on the trail of the elusive Beber even as I lay there under the dirty thatch.

"People will worry," I say to Nok. "I must make a telephone call."

"They have phones in Turkey, don't they, Alfred?" Henshaw will say. "Do you have any idea the concern you have caused. We all pictured you lying in a pasture somewhere, or weighted down with cement somewhere in the middle of the Bosporus."

"Telephone far from here," she ventures. "I can go. I call for you."

Oh dear. Oh dear. How little this girl grasps of the ordeal for which she has signed on. Buber the Magnificent is not the perspiring little chap lying on a mat at her feet.

———⌘———

("That's strange," Nigel will have said to my secretary. He is concerned about my protracted absence, has called her to ask for information. "He told me you would have his itinerary if I needed to reach him."

"There must be some misunderstanding," she will reply. "He told me to get in touch with you if I needed him for some reason."

I don't know how Nigel would put it all together, so surreptitious was I, but I expect that eventually he would. I can see his face as he disembarks at the airport, makes his way through the

103

drumming heat and the gauntlet of drivers and touts standing at the entrance. I see his face as he is bounced around in the back of the old taxi, watches through the window the toll taker standing in a plume of exhaust, watches as the car passes the temples and the billboards, being offered all manner of sexual adventure himself, hotly declining. Nigel isn't one for a great deal of strangeness, not one to spend much time in the sunlight. He will brush things over with Lysol before he touches them, will find his nose wrinkling simply by reflex, will sit crouched on the seat of a sputtering samlor, an eyebrow raised, a handkerchief at his mouth. In this search for his missing nephew he has already reached a number of conclusions he wishes he had never been forced to; now confronts the dirt, the tumult, the noise, with a mix of stoicism and sadness.

He will cotton on to what has been going on before too long, well before some young consulate official explains to him in the most explicit terms what might account for all the secrecy, if not for my disappearance. Coil by coil it has already unraveled until it has all lain quite bare, is quite explicable. My corpse is shamed, my memory is an embarrassment.

But then, if there is any place where the compulsions of the flesh are irrelevant it must be in the grave. Please let it be.)

———

It takes several more days before I am able to leave. I have eaten nothing but soup, bits of animal, clumps of rice that I insist be boiled to death before I will touch it. I am recovered but still shaken and uncertain.

"Tomorrow I must go," I tell her. "Do you know when I can catch the train?"

"I come with you," she says and for a moment, lying there with my head in her lap, this all seems quite reasonable, that she would accompany me, sit beside me on the train, back to the city.

"But I must go home," I say. "To America. To my business."

She says nothing, places one hand on my head as if to feel my thoughts, another on my shoulder. What is she thinking, I wonder, this girl in tan trousers and a white tee shirt, her Buddha amulet hanging from her neck and brushing over me each time she leans forward? Her face is inscrutable, far away.

Her face is lovely.

"No problem," she says. "I wait you in city."

My heart is breaking for her and I am panic-struck. I have scraped something from the murky bottom of all endeavor, transformed it into an entertaining quest, and now I am on the precipice of causing real damage. She will accept it, of course, whatever it is I dish out, this I can see already, add it to the tray of things that she has seen and had to do, the contemptible bald man from America who has taken her for a fool, but that is not what I want. Not how I want to behave.

"I don't want you to go back to the Star of Love Bar," I say, and as I say it I could slap myself for the banality of the sentiment.

("What else should she do?" Nigel asks. "Become a doctor, perhaps? A lawyer?")

She looks up and out into the trees. I have no idea what she is thinking. Ten days ago she had clean forgotten who I was, that I had ever existed save for the well-thumbed little book I bought her on a whim; and now I have barged, bought, vomited my way right into the heart of everything she knows.

"I can help you," I say. "What is it that you really want to do in your life? Maybe I can help."

And I mean it. Perhaps I can do something of value, Santa Buber, spread a little of Henshaw & Potter's bounty this way and sweep the girl out of waywardness and into an unimpeachable respectability. She begins to rub my shoulders, my neck, the base of my scalp. For a while she says nothing, continues looking into the air, remains lost in thought. Finally she answers:

"I wait you," she says.

———∞∞∞———

There is a small town about two hours away if one goes by truck, and that is how we go, she and I sitting on mats in the flatbed of an aging Toyota. She has negotiated this one, protected me, somehow managed a price of seven dollars for a trip of sixty miles over packed mud roads. From time to time I catch the driver's eye as he checks on his payload, see him look into the mirror to scrutinize his portly little piece of cargo and its lissome companion. At some hotel in Europe or the Caribbean they will ask after the preferences of my niece, don't you think, reveling richly in the joke of it, a subtle jab at the purchase of wealth. Now the truck driver, a thin muscular boy, stares unabashedly and there is something of envy, something of contempt, in his eyes.

We are dropped in front of a hotel and after the roughness of the village it seems, all of a sudden, as if this shabby provincial building has comforts that surpass anything I could ever have hoped for. There are telephones, showers, bedside tables, hard blue carpeting, stained and musty admittedly, but carpeting nonetheless. We are shown to our room by a porter, a boy dressed smartly in the hotel's colors, and as he draws the curtains back I see that we look out onto fields that might seem to others to be unspeakably picturesque except that I know better. I have just come from them and find nothing in them that is either serene or comforting.

"I have to use the telephone," I say to her and she reacts as if she has not heard me, stands at the window, looks out into the field.

I put my fingers to my lips.

"While I talk, please no talk," I say, and she nods.

How to ensure, is the question, that a line from here, from a hotel in this ramshackle little town smack in the middle of nowhere, will appear to be a line from Ankara? I lean against a bureau and rub my face, wonder how it could be, what defect deep within me exists to create such a situation. Could the wavy-haired good fellows with their curvy wives and healthy children who romp about on the grass at Henshaw & Potter's annual picnic even conceive of it?

"Henshaw & Potter," a voice at the end of the line chirps.

It is Anna, the receptionist. She has been with the firm as long as I have. She is unmarried, they say, a habitué of a whole gamut of singles events. Hers is a face I have dreaded seeing on the edge of a ballroom in some squalid suburban hotel.

"I'll put you right through, Mr. Buber," she says.

It is a strange feeling to be talking to her from this room so far away from the life I am known to lead.

"Mr. Buber's office," my secretary says, and when she hears it is me she exclaims, "Mr. Buber! You were supposed to be back last week. I was on the verge of calling your home to find out whether you were back in town, but then I figured you were probably having such an interesting trip you decided to extend it. You sound as clear as if you were in the next room."

I look around the room, the one in which I am standing, and picture her at her desk back there in the other life. On the dressing table I have laid out my little pharmacy to inventory its contents. On the table next to my bed is a book on Turkey. I have thumbed through it just in case I am asked questions.

"How are you enjoying your trip?" she asks brightly. "Is it everything you expected?"

"More so," I answer. "I'll tell you all about it when I get back."

"People here do envy you," she says, "and certainly nothing's happened that can't wait until your return. Mr. Henshaw did stop by and ask for the telephone number of your hotel and when would be the best time to reach you. He has a question?"

"I'd rather not," I say. "I *am* supposed to be on vacation. Can't they breathe over there without me?"

"I know," she says. "When will you be back?"

"I can't say," I tell her. "I am having such a fine time that I may extend it another couple of days."

My secretary, a spry woman in her late fifties, says that she will continue to cover for me and I replace the receiver. (I do not believe in heaven or hell, not anymore, and yet this turns out to be so easy, so effortless, that one wonders whether it is possible, just perhaps, that there are some sins for which, if one is careful, there is no penalty.) I look up, relieved that this is now behind me, and am surprised to see that a new sadness has descended on Nok. She is sitting on the side of the bed looking quite dejected.

"What's the matter?" I ask.

She says nothing but I can see she is formulating a question, is not sure how to ask it.

"What?" I say, concerned.

"Your wife, that one?" she asks, pointing at the phone. "That lady your wife?"

"For heaven's sake, no," I say, and I cannot avoid saying it with a laugh. "No no no. That was my secretary. I don't have a wife."

"*Seclety*?" she says.

"Secretary," I repeat, and then I play at charades with her, type into the air, answer an imaginary telephone, all to no avail.

"I her boss," I say finally, and this she seems to understand though she is by no means reassured.

"If your wife," she says, finally, "no problem for me."

What is it with her, with this twilight world into which I have invited myself? We have now spent a week together, Nok and I, inseparably one could say, and yet oddly enough we have not been alone before, not ever, not in the village, not in the Star of Love Bar. There is something quite awkward in it now, she and I from our respective corners of life trapped in a room that feels somehow desolate with no bar girls or relatives or cows nuzzling about. She is small now, smaller than at any other time, has no context other than as my purchase, would not be here at all if it were not for me. She says nothing, does not move, suggests nothing by her presence. She is, in short, Buber's to do with as he pleases and yet mark this, the irony of this, the laughable irony of this: Of desire the Buber feels none. He would rather be in a library reading periodicals from exotic places (thinking of women like this, I should add), than here, would rather be at home and sitting in one of his strange gilt chairs, than on this bed. He must possess desire, he must, but without warning it has slipped into its own inaccessible place.

Allow me to venture into territory so unfamiliar it is *chutzpah* that I be there at all. She is wearing denim jeans and a white shirt, I tell you, that and clunky black shoes that come to a sharp point in the front, have a large buckle holding nothing across the top, are somehow truncated at the back. They are very unattractive, mark her as a farm girl lost amidst the offerings of the city, someone who pairs things that do not belong together. Her thick, ropey hair is stacked atop her head, coiled over within itself so that it perches like a snake with its final coil trilling gently in the air-conditioned air. She has a plastic purse on her lap, clear on one side, pink on the other. In it are lipstick, keys — though to what I don't know, a cell phone that she has said is deactivated, and a red wallet with banknotes and a few coins. She is a mixed metaphor so profound I cannot take it all in, a peasant who five more years in the fields will have turned wizened and middle-aged, a struggling young woman, a compassionate friend if the last few days are anything to go by, a girl among dozens in a bar. Her face is covered with a vague sheen of perspiration after our long ride, her lips are full and quite naturally pink, her teeth are white. It is too hot to feel desire, the situation is too incongruous to feel desire, and yet somehow in the heat itself — perhaps the heat itself — is an animal force. It is too hot to make love in this room, could be almost suicidal, and yet one cannot not desire this woman, ignore the slender wrists, the cotton fabric of the shirt, the sparkling eyes. One cannot. Everything in its place and a place for everything, but then somehow the simmering presence of desire becomes unmistakable, prickles, raises itself, stirs, settles back.

She smooths a bead of dew on a glass of iced water she is holding, looks at me, looks away without expectation. There is a single stain on the collar of her blouse. My own clothes are damp with perspiration. Hers are dry.

And still I have not touched her.

I walk across to her and kiss her and of course she yields, kisses me back, and it is surprising to be confronted so immediately with the intimacy of a stranger. There is something peppery to it, something minty, a touch of sourness. (I have never before this moment kissed a woman on the mouth. Rebecca has not cared for it, the others have never allowed it; and though perhaps in some long lost time that woman from Golders Green may have done something similar, I have no memory of it, thankfully.) She stands there in the middle of the room, so much smaller than I, so much thinner, reaches up and puts her arms around me, parts her lips, both submits and responds. I lose my heart to her in this instant, to her earnestness, her generosity, her presence. I do not want this to stop because I know, I am certain, that things rest on an uncertain fulcrum, that whatever comes next gets made up as it happens, that whatever in this moment is clean and good is for this moment only.

She pulls away.

"I go bathroom," she says, and as she walks away my misgivings are confirmed. Everything is temporary, of course it is. Moments come and go. Intimacy must be earned. It does not simply descend. She is and she isn't mine to do with as I please. Her affection is and isn't what it seems to be. I can immerse myself in it all if I choose, but she will not, because her vagueness, her submission exist within boundaries so firmly scribed, it is as if it has all been hardwired. One can lose one's head to an intimacy that is not fickle but that is not genuine either, a love that is encompassing but that contains nothing of substance.

I hear flushing, running water, more flushing. Time passes and I continue to wait as things clack around in the bathroom, water is splashed, cabinets open and close. Finally she emerges, her clothes folded and stacked on the bathroom floor, she wrapped firmly in a hotel towel. She pauses by the door, smiles, then walks to the bed and slips under the covers with the towel still wrapped about her.

"Are you okay?" I ask for no particular reason other than to hear something from her, some reassurance that this is, after all, more than mechanical, that she is, after all, not simply submitting because she has been bargained for in a deal struck by my representative Pla and her father.

"Okay," she says, an edge of impatience in her voice. "You come here."

After a week in which she has seemed wholly present, filled with compassion, a week in which there has been a glimmer of an understanding between us, she is mine now, but not mine either. The part of her that has been most freely surrendered to a host of other men is all she yields. She gestures, leads, shows what I am expected to do, how I am to be serviced, is wary, quiet, almost, one could say, uninvolved. I possess her but it feels that I am in her debt, liable at any moment to feel her disengage, to lose something I never had in the first place. She is there, but she is not there.

In short, she submits so entirely that it is as if she is not there at all.

That is not what I meant at all.

That is not it, at all.

Then again, what was the Buber expecting, sexual athlete that he is.

When I am done I spring from the bed and carry my little pharmacy into the bathroom, and gargle so furiously with undiluted peroxide that I burn the lining of my mouth. I scrub and ointment, disinfect and shower, soak. As I wash I look in the dirty mirror and see something I would rather not see, my pate, the folds of my stomach, my hairless leg up on the counter. I scrub and examine as if the flora of HIV will burst from my skin and take me down in an instant. I am unclean.

It is a fitful night really, how could it not be, and not only because there are remnants of the fever in my blood, chills that will take weeks fully to resolve. It is a night filled with dreams and incoherent images, the rustling of a stranger in the bed beside me. From the street come strange noises. Shadows flit about the walls. Nok shudders as she sleeps.

I lean against the headboard and watch her carefully, her long black hair spread over the pillows, one slender leg stretched out above the sheet. She has an artist's hands, really, not a farmer's, thin wrists, narrow shoulders. Her skin is dark, heavily tanned, and there are already traces of creases on her forehead, at the edges of her eyes, at the bridge of her nose. They are, if anything, endearing. I wonder what she will do when her looks have faded, whether, in her village or elsewhere, there is a boy who will be willing to marry someone with her history. She is one of thousands, hundreds of thousands, of country girls who migrate into the beds of foreign men and then slink back, fade into the countryside forever.

When I am old, when I am done with her, I will see pictures of wrinkled Asian farm women, and I will wonder what became of her.

———

From there the rest unfolds all on its own, almost as if having set in motion the forces I have there is little choice left in it. It is not comfortable, even in this barren town where nothing is familiar, being so obviously, so notoriously, a customer of the young girl at my side. Walking beside me she seems very small, hardly of the same species, much too fragile and graceful, how else to put it, there amidst the pungency, the litter of cabbage leaves and broken crates, a dead animal lying trampled at the edge of a drain, a noise that drowns out her words when she tries to say something, swallows my reply.

It must look so odd, I think, so out of place in any normal scheme of things, for this beautiful girl to be walking down an alley followed, two steps behind, by a large foreigner with a pack strapped to his waist, with beads of perspiration coating the top of his head. She steps around the obstructions—a plank, a puddle, a mound of dirty rice—and he follows, soundlessly, still two steps behind. Nobody knows us but they are human beings, after all, must take it in, the incongruity, the obvious nature of the exchange. It is vulgar, it must be regardless of the idiom, not only a vague murmur of Nigel's that makes it so, a threatened laugh from the young women at Henshaw & Potter.

Her black shoes scrape the pavement, the edges of her hair fly back, she narrows her eyes against the gusts of smoke. The people are animated, trim, self-possessed, make their way among the obstacles as if they were nothing worth obsessing about, as if Nok and I were nothing worth obsessing about, the simple detritus of life.

"Where you like to eat?" she asks.

"You choose," I say, but it occurs to me that I have no idea what this girl eats, for heaven's sake, what she finds appetizing and what she does not.

Flies buzz about stagnant puddles in the road, hover over discarded pieces of vegetable.

⁂

We spend the day in the little town, catch an evening bus back to the city. We have returned to the bedroom and been intimate again, the second time different than the first, less urgent, less strange. On the bus she sits beside me and looks out the window, a small person, almost inanimate at times, with sweet-smelling hair, a slender golden hand resting on my knee. It is not easy to talk but there is now something of an understanding between us, vague, incoherent, illogical. We are together now, are treated as if we are together, have in some completely unexpected way developed a shared history, have made love, twice, showered together, eaten together, share an uncertainty as to what can follow from what has now firmly begun.

As we approach the city—the fields seem suddenly to become littered, crowded with buildings, abandoned pieces of machinery, large blotches of barren mud—she begins paying close attention to the scenes passing by the window. She watches a gold-spired temple as we approach, looks back as it recedes, draws my attention to something—it appears there has been a motorcycle accident at the edge of the road—and then drops her hand back onto my leg without comment.

The traffic thickens, passengers around us show signs of agitation, the air outside becomes tinged with a copper haze.

"When you go home?" she asks.

"I think tomorrow," I say. "If I can get a ticket."

She takes this in, sits for a few moments, appears to be thinking.

"Lady from telephone," she says at last. "She meet you?"

"Listen to me," I say, and I begin to laugh, but I see that for her this is no laughing matter. "That lady works for me. I am her boss. Only her boss."

I am bound to this girl by something as fragile as smoke. If she were to lose sight of me in a crowd she would not find me again.

"When you come back?" she asks.

If I get off the bus, return to my hotel, get my bags, go to the airport, I can flee without a trace, morph back into the Buber I am without so much as a chrysalis to show for it. But that Buber has been eclipsed by another. I don't mind that this girl, this child, chooses to feel possessive, wants to know the when's and the how's of it. I feel, take this or leave it, oddly peaceful.

"I will come back," I say, "before too long."

I mean it when I say it. I mean it, honestly. I will go back to where I belong, and sitting in my white ice chamber I will think this through, process what has happened, figure out a way to merge my life as it has been with this detour I have taken, this excursion gone wrong, gone right, that has filled a void that haunted and haunted without reprise. The risks, the costs, of doing so will be enormous, are obvious; but there is, there must be, something to be said for the sense — as I sit on the bus, covered in dust, jittering through a landscape so alien I could be on the moon — that I am not unhappy.

I mean it when I say it.

Pla sits on a stool beside the door. When she sees us approaching she shouts, jumps up, runs towards us. Nok comes to life as well in a way she has not since we left her village. Her face changes, becomes animated as she rattles away in her own language, laughs, appears perfectly carefree. I know they are talking about me because they glance across at me from time to time and also, God help me, because Nok holds my hand especially tightly, somewhat, one could say, triumphantly.

Be that as it may.

"Good man," Pla says to me, making a thumbs-up gesture.

"I don't know about that," I mumble, Buberlike, embarrassed.

"No. Good," Pla says after a while, and now I feel an edge of unease, that once again little fish mouth is manipulating, engineering. "You take care her. You go home, pay money, take care her."

Things are being assumed here, of course, that have not been agreed upon. Even as I know that I will have to do something, make some arrangement that will allow Nok to stay off her knees before foreign men, I am wary. The line between being generous and being taken for a fool is a smudgy one. I do not welcome the aggression of the demand, the raucous way it has been presented. I bristle, and Nok, sensing a shift in the atmosphere, says something.

Pla, chastened, retreats.

"I sorry," she says. "I sorry for Pla."

"It's okay," I say.

As I walk from the hotel to the waiting car, I see a man who has accosted me several times on my prior visit. He has said his name is Boon, presents himself as a schoolteacher, and insists that in offering all manner of expeditions and merchandise he is simply trying to improve his English. I have shrugged him off each time, but there has been something in his humor that has been engaging.

Tonight, in good humor myself, I stop.

"Hold on one moment," I say to Nok as I cross over to him.

"Boon?" I say.

"Yes," he says.

He pauses and then he smiles broadly.

"Alfred. From the United States."

"You have a good memory," I say, and then because I can't help it I add conspiratorially "You're not a school teacher at all. You're a scoundrel."

He laughs and laughs.

"Of course I am. Certainly I am," he says. "A person can be both."

He is about to say something more, but then at the same moment we both turn and he sees Nok, turns back to me.

"I see you've made the most of your stay," he says. "Very lovely. Very lovely indeed."

"It's easy to start," I say. "Not easy to stop."

"Very true," he says. "It's a danger of the place."

"I went to her village, you know," I say, for whatever reason needing to tell someone, the last person I will tell for quite some time. "I think I may have married her, in one way or another."

"You are not the first one," he says. "I will give you some advice if you like."

"What's that?" I ask, curious.

"Get on your airplane and forget," he says. "If you come back, you start again."

"It's too late for that," I say and Boon, regrouping, laughs it off and calls after me: "You want to buy *Lolex*?"

CHAPTER FIVE

A consummate liar, this Buber, holding forth on the glories of places he has never set a tasseled, dust-caked, foot upon.

"The Topkapi Palace is a must see," he babbles. "Architecture and mosaics like nothing one can imagine. Of course the palace harem is a place one could spend the rest of one's life."

I have handed her a wad of bills, two thousand dollars' worth, at the last possible moment. The envelope bulges, barely holds.

"It okay," she says, her voice uncertain, her fingers not quite grasping what I have handed her. "You pay father already."

"This is for you," I say. "A gift."

She holds the envelope, but barely. A bus comes roaring by and we both step back. She covers her eyes as a whirlwind of dust swirls our way. It subsides and she lowers her arm, looks across at me, thinks for a moment before speaking.

"This mean," she says softly, "that you say goodbye forever."

Oh no, the Buber, assures her. Oh no.

Could it be, is it possible, that the face I see in my bathroom mirror wears a slightly self-satisfied smirk, has an air of complacency that was lacking before? I stand there and ponder this, whether it can indeed be possible that there are no consequences to things, even to things that are foul and taboo, that but for his own weakness even that mopey drip Raskolnikov would have gotten clean away. The deeper my transgression goes, the more complex and involved and long lasting, the lighter about it I feel. I have crossed the line, and crossed it further, and all that has happened is that with distance an air of pettiness has descended on my misgivings.

I have been careful in the past not to keep evidence of my contemptible hobbies, but this time I return with an incriminating little cache of mementos that I want to keep close at hand, that I want the luxury of referring to, looking at, having. Most important of these is Nok's gift, a grassy little construct which she presented to me on the backseat of the taxi as it idled outside the airport terminal. I have surprised her by telling her that she cannot come inside and so she hands it to me in the car, prods me to unwrap it right then. She has tried to anticipate my tastes, stood beside me as I looked over a display of mediocre watercolors in the hotel lobby, has chosen for me from a curio stand a picture of sorts, brown grass woven into black velvet, high-lit with luminous paint.

I thank her, instruct the driver to take her wherever she pleases, and with no further ceremony the car pulls away. There is something vulnerable in how sharply her head jolts as the driver swerves into the traffic.

—✧—

I have held forth so well on the trilling wonders of Paris and the ruins of Istanbul that if I chose, my excursions may scarcely have happened at all; but I cannot bring myself to destroy Nok's gift. Would it be odd to say that it is, back in my austere house, an object of warmth and value? I tuck it all, the brochures and the receipts, Nok's gift, under old income tax returns in my closet. The knowledge that my little stash is there confirms, feeds, this strange new smug-ness, this sense that all those things that have been so long out of reach, the freshness and the liveliness of it, the seduc-tive eyes, flickering lips, the things reserved for others, are now of less account. I, Buber, have weaned myself from them, have something instead, something that will serve as a substitute.

Right!

But there *is* the matter of this strange new energy, some-thing I sense will not simply dissipate with time. Perhaps it will vent with a brisk walk, maybe even a jog. As I place my little bundle in the closet, I lay my hands on a pair of almost brittle sneakers and haul them out, find a pair of shorts, a tee shirt so old I can't remember ever having worn it.

Not since I was a child locked in the backseat of the Morris for seemingly endless drives to Bulawayo have I been so restless, excited in a way I had almost forgotten, filled with an overabundance of energy. They would say, the muscular young women at Henshaw & Potter of whom I am so solicitous, that I have been dishonest, that I have taken something that is not mine, but then they have the power of youth and of beauty, of being desired, and I have only that of the wallet, that and of a wile I did not expect.

The gardener looks up from his flowerbed, watches as I prance about at the far end of the garden, returns head down to his own thoughts.

One doesn't need to be a genius to guess at them.

The worst of it, it seems, is that I have no one in whom I can confide. A temptation to share something of it is present, to tell *something* of it to *someone,* but of course that would be a mistake. Of course I won't do it. Nigel asks about my recent travels, listens carefully, solicits descriptions of the various things I purport to have seen.

"I must say," he says at last, "you're a careful observer. A civilized man through and through."

"Thank you, Nigel," I say. "I'm finding, strangely enough, that I feel most myself in the most unlikely of places."

Nigel looks at me skeptically, lowers his cup.

"I'm not sure whether that's a good or a bad thing," he says. "One has to live life as one is, not as one isn't."

"What are you saying?" I ask.

I don't like it when he pontificates. There's a judgmental edge to it, as if there's some sort of object lesson for me in whatever it is he's saying.

"You are who you are," he says, "wherever you are. Feeling liberated by being where you aren't known carries its own risks."

I'm still not sure what he's getting at, whether he's hinting that he knows that things aren't as I depict them.

"I'm not sure I would use the word liberated," I say. "It's simply that the constraints of one's life are lessened when one isn't surrounded by entrenched expectations."

"It is those expectations that give one perspective," Nigel says. "Men particularly aren't built to live alone, to travel alone. I don't know why it is, but it just is, that men need the leavening influence of women. There are women out there, Alfred, many women, and I can't help but believe that if you were open to it you'd find one to your liking."

I look around the room with its delicate ornaments, its doilies over the arms of each chair, its faded velvet fabrics. Nigel once lived in Rhodesia too, and though he left when he was still a boy, bits and pieces of it remain in him. This little Victorian setup of his—the patterned China plates, the formality of his table, the porcelain shepherdess on the mantle—are all quite redolent of life in Salisbury.

"Oh, I don't know," I say, twirling a knife or a napkin or whatever is before me. "You can live a perfectly reasonable life alone."

"You can, of course," Nigel replies, "but it is much harder. Men have a tendency to lose perspective when left to their own devices. That's just my view, mind you, but I would be misleading you if I didn't worry about this wanderlust of yours, whether you're looking for something you aren't more likely to find closer to home."

I look across his table at him—he is a short man, ruddy, with a profusion of white hair on his head, at his eyebrows, bursting from his nose and ears—and I have the sense that he and I are not, at the heart of it, as dissimilar as we might appear to be, that he has made his choices, faced his temptations, compromised in ways that might feel familiar to me were I ever to know the details of it all.

Nigel is stolid, stoic, an astute observer.

"I'm fine, Nigel," I assure him, "perfectly fine." But when I leave his house the thought of returning to my icy cell is intolerable, and I turn instead towards another part of town, to places where you are best served by keeping your expectations quite plain.

My neighbors had become quite serious about the alderman issue when I returned from that second visit to Asia. A small delegation of townspeople went so far as to visit me at Henshaw & Potter in an attempt to persuade me. There was a vacancy on the board, they reported, possibly the swing vote for an expanded library, better paid teachers, a town art program.

Of course I wasn't going to do it, then less than ever, though I was less categorical in my response than I actually felt.

"There are others much more politically astute than I am," I remember saying to a room of vigorously shaking heads. "I lack the instincts for it, but I will try to be of service to whoever does decide to do this."

"Oh no, Mr. Buber. You would be perfect. You have no vested interests, for one thing. And you're so, well, elegant in how you present your opinions."

"No, no," I say, and I am blushing, whether from the praise or from a glimpse, just a glimpse, of a basket on the floor, an ox cart, a house on stilts, I cannot say. "I'm not your man."

They leave dejected, still respectful, pause to examine the artwork in the elevator lobby.

"Beautiful old offices," someone says, and I agree. Buber in his crypt, wood-paneled, austere, ever so tasteful. "She suck you."

It wasn't so much that I fretted about discovery, though that was undeniably a concern. It was something else too now.

I actually didn't care.

Their library be darned.

—∞∞—

Not an alderman, but round the grounds twice on Monday, two-and-a-half times on Tuesday. I instruct my housekeeper on a new diet regimen, meals laced with broccoli and spinach, light on red meat. I venture into a health food store, exit carrying a bag filled with extracts of laughable things.

"To be honest with you," the housekeeper says, "I don't know how to cook this way."

She's a muscular Irish woman, Mrs. Savage, who drives in each morning and makes no secret of her likes and dislikes.

"They say it's supposed to be healthy," she says, "and maybe it is. But why would you want to eat like this?'

"I'm not too particular," I say. "Just boil it all and save the broth."

"Broth you call it. It'll be more like dishwater." And then she relents. "It's your stomach," she says. "It's your house."

I stand naked at the mirror and examine it all, the unprepossessing stomach, the little pouch of a chin, the exact dimensions of this or that fringe of hair. Each morning, now, a rendezvous with the scale, a sizing up of the body before a mirror, all without apology. A set of new suits, glove soft shoes, a spiffy selection of ties.

"What happened to you in Europe, Alf?" Henshaw asks. "You've come back a changed man."

"How so?" I ask.

I know, of course I know, what he's after, but I make him say it anyway.

"This new look of yours," he says. "Upbeat manner, fancy ties, the rest of it. If I were to guess I'd say there was a female of the species involved."

"Now whatever would make you say that?" I ask with feigned innocence.

"You're not the only one who's been to France, you know," Henshaw says, confusing even where I have just been, reducing to irrelevance my series of careful alibis. "As I recall, I was introduced to a French woman or two myself."

I allow a knowing smile, leave the rest unsaid.

In the men's room I look at myself closely in the mirror. Perhaps the shape of my face is changing. My cheeks seem to have become more angular giving me a slightly haughty air, perhaps that or a hungry one, but either way change is good, breaks old patterns. My hair is no longer closely cropped, has become *Shakespeherian*, Elizabethan. It flaps against my neck as I run, flap, flap, flap, in time with my new satin shorts, my running shoes, the little ankle meter calibrating how far I have gone.

I'm up to three times round the grounds, soon will qualify for a canter through the town where my fans and political supporters can witness the transformation for themselves. I am aware of every nuance in this process of change but that is not, of course, true of others. Henshaw has made his remark, settled back into his old apparent regard for me. Others seem scarcely to have noticed.

I run, shower, groom, powder, go to bed each night as crisp and fragrant as a new lettuce.

—∞∞∞—

I stand at the sink alone and not alone, awash in the sense that someone else may be present, someone ethereal, someone who could be conjured up in an instant and yet who seems barely to exist at all. I have tried to write to her, have started several times and then abandoned the attempt.

I find myself writing as if to a child.

> *"It is very cold here, not like you are used to. I like this weather. I don't think you would."*

"What did you expect?" Nigel would say. "Relatively speaking, she is a child."

I think, one afternoon as I step from my office to hand a note to my secretary and look down to see a line of secretaries sitting at their desks, that this is a sight I have seen a thousand times but never carefully. They look like nothing so much as galley slaves out there in the hall, their heads bobbing mindlessly as they enter, hour after hour, figures, meaningless words, inflated concepts into their blinking terminals. They will tell you, any one of the Henshaw & Potter women if asked, about the drudgery of it.

And drudgery it is, now of a particularly oppressive kind. I am constantly on the verge of throwing it all over, selling everything, cutting all ties and immersing myself in a world of my own creation. I could make it my life's mission to protect Nok from men like myself, to make her life a paradise. At dusk in that other place one sees lines of girls sitting like divas in beauty shop chairs, stylists behind them working to wash and fix their hair for the evening, watching themselves carefully in mirrors. They comment, gesture, sit in silence. There is a measure of pride on some of their faces, no squalor, some sadness, a quiet acceptance. There are no computer terminals but the heads are the same, the row of women's heads intent on their respective tasks.

Could it be that, separated though our lives are by oceans and whatever else, life itself is not so disparate that between her and me there cannot be coincidences? Her father is stubborn and eccentric, a *luftmensch* in his own way, though of course not a Jewish Communist. There is a compliant mother, a childhood spent mostly listening, unflattering images of oneself. The planet is, after all, a finite place.

"Were you a virgin when you came to the city?" I have asked. "When you started at the Star of Love Bar?"

"No," she says, and with such reticence that Buber the Marauder cannot help but continue, needs to tease it from her and then to apply the balm, himself, oh so tenderly, oh so lovingly.

"You had a boyfriend in your village?" he asks.

"No," she says simply. "My father friend."

Even Buber knows to leave it where it is.

I stand a jade Buddha on the corner of my desk and it's there for a week before my secretary notices it.

"I didn't know they had jade in Turkey," she says.

"They probably don't," I say. "It must have come from somewhere else."

"It's very attractive," she says, gathering papers from the box and organizing them into a pile.

I am so filled with energy, so easily tired.

Life doesn't stop, of course.

"I have an announcement," Arthur Henshaw tells a specially convened meeting of the partners.

As usual there are hors d'oeuvres on a table against the wall, carafes filled with sherry.

"Some of you will welcome it," he adds, a wry smile playing across his face, "say that it is long overdue, in fact. Others will view it with hesitation."

The long and the short of it is that he is retiring. It's unclear exactly why, and he discourages all speculation, but his decision is final and his departure imminent. There are a few days of skirmishes as the rest of us try to decide how we are going to run the firm without its founder. Some of the younger hotheads come up with a range of ideas several of us find quite unsettling. The whole firm feels unsettled, in fact, with meetings behind closed doors and a collection of factions seeking to form alliances. It is unseemly and it is laced with all manner of unspoken threats and silent menace.

Henshaw calls us in for another meeting and warns us that while it may seem as if an institution like ours can endure forever, the whole thing is also quite fragile. I agree with that sentiment wholeheartedly, but having made his own plans clear it is as if Arthur Henshaw has, suddenly and quite without reason, lost most of his powers of suasion.

"I am sorry, Alfred," he says to me privately. "This does promise to be more unruly than either of us would have liked."

I'm not sure what the hotheads have in mind, though there is something about their attitude I do not like at all. I throw in my lot with several of the older fellows and end up being proposed for the management committee. We have the votes and so it is.

I am to succeed my old mentor. There was a time when such a development would have meant a great deal to me.

Dear Nok: I very important person now.

⸛

I still run each evening, follow the old bike path through the town, complete a routine that ends each time behind a plate of defrosted food at my solitary glass table. It seems as if I am destined to settle into a new groove I am wearing for myself, and that any prospect for change is bound to be ephemeral and elusive. Doing anything else, taking what I have begun and following it through to its end, is a vision that each time I seek it, evaporates into smoke.

⸛

And just what, pray tell, were that great explorer, the law firm entrepreneur Alfred Buber, to bring Nok back to his world with him . . . what would she do once the wonderment was over? What would she *do*, once his leave had ended, the time had come for him to return to his great place in the city, there amidst the querulous glances and oblique questions of his colleagues? Something tells me she will sleep a lot, turn night into day, that she will make free use of the television and the telephone. When she wakes she will wash, dress, potter about for a while, savor her first hours, her first days, alone among the great porcelain vases and walls of silk.

She will open and close things, take pieces of food from the great chrome refrigerator, examine herself in a mirror. She may stroll out onto the grass, contemplate the street outside. Perhaps she will dare to venture further, to the little town with its quaint stores and everyone-knows-everyone air, the money I foisted on her tucked tightly into the pocket of her new down jacket. She will peck at it all—like Robinson Crusoe or Gulliver, like Buber himself on that vulgar street where he found her—wondering what to make of it, where to make her foray.

"You're Mr. Buber's guest," a store owner will say. "Can I show you something specific?"

She may choose something, something trivial, hold out a handful of bills, carry what she has bought back to the house and lay it carefully on the bed. She will show it proudly to the bwana when he returns from his great place in the city at dusk. I picture her sitting in one of my silent rooms as I do battle with the upstarts in the city, watching Mrs. Savage as she vacuums. Nok will lift her brown feet into the air as the machine sweeps by, lower them when it whirs off into another room. I cannot leave her like that, can I, sitting motionless on a couch? She is not simply a decoration. She is a person, and while you could say that she is bought and paid for, indentured, has no options, surely basic decency requires that I give her a further gift, work to insert her slowly but honestly into her new environment.

I swivel in my armchair, look out my office door and down the carpeted hall of Henshaw & Potter. I must plan a life for this illusion of mine, this girl and her basket still waiting for me across the world. There are language courses she could take, must take, classes in history, nursing even,

whatever else it is she might fancy. I will make the necessary arrangements for her, she will wonder at her fortune, at
this apocalyptic transformation. I will drop her at the door
of her new institute, watch as she goes carrying her new
books, her new satchel, wearing her new clothes, listen carefully as she practices her homework each evening.

"The rain in Spain falls mainly on the plain."

She will make friends too, doubtless, and it is here that
my vision runs into trouble, becomes derailed, refuses to
cooperate.

"I be a little late tonight, Alfie," she says. "One of the
student having party."

I could go, of course, stand around with youngsters half
my age listening to rock and roll and drinking beer out of
a keg. Or I could stay away. Either way it is not possible
that she won't be noticed, a beautiful young girl in fetching
clothes, fresh skinned, chaste, there courtesy of a deluded
old fool who has snatched her from a bordello and stands
squeamishly in a corner between two youngsters who ignore
him, or waiting in the suburbs for her to return. One of the
boys, slouching there against the wall in his baggy jeans and
carefully frayed tee shirt, turns to her and says something,
repeats himself, elicits a coy smile. She covers her mouth
with her hand, pretends to be shocked, allows him to continue. This Clare Quilty, this thief, will want to snatch what
is not his, to work his youthful and devious ways to snatch
the dream I have built from air and yearning, and I will
have no recourse.

Amazing, really. He envies some mythic youngster with
his hands in his pockets while ten thousand miles away men
pay a pittance for the privilege of possessing her entirely.
Even so, what I have begun shows no signs of abating,
emerges from time to time from its own dark corridor to
present possibilities and choices that could not, surely, survive in the cold light of the day.

———

And so it is that Buber becomes head of one of the most
elegant firms in the city, a compromise candidate, perhaps,

but elected nonetheless, indisputably legitimate, grudgingly congratulated. I notice—who could not—the group that files silently from the conference room when the results are announced, but then change is seldom universally and unequivocally welcomed. One must find middle ground, I have said. One must be prepared to compromise.

Filling the shoes of someone you have come to admire greatly is not a simple matter. I decline, when offered, the opportunity to move into Henshaw's office, for instance, and not only because it seems presumptuous. There is a tenuous feel to things and you do not wish to tempt fate. I am keenly aware, even as I move to take charge, that there is a faction that is far from happy with the way things have turned out.

But I am determined to make the most of it, to disprove the doubters. Those who have allied themselves with me, the old guard if you will, are sound men, men of good judgment. We will allay the fears, maintain the ship. What has worked in the past will work in the future, of this I have no doubt, and for me of course there is, at first, the more personal mission, to continue what Arthur Henshaw began, to make seamless a transition which, once it is accomplished, will seem to have been logical and even compelled. Long days in the office, under the circumstances, are for me a beneficial matter. You cannot spend too much of your time mired in matters of the flesh, in indiscretions past and contemplated, when you have a business to run, spreadsheets to evaluate, personnel matters to mediate.

I have to concede that for all the frenzy, the new importance I seem to have acquired, people constantly at my office door seeking advice on this or that, I cannot shake the feeling that I am out of my depth, a humbug so to speak, this portly little Jewish chap out of Southern Rhodesia purporting to direct one of the city's venerable institutions.

"Shall we subcontract out our copying requirements, Mr. Buber?"

I care, and I don't care. I want to succeed even as I know that success will create no change in the sameness of the hermetic evenings that bring each day to an end. Even worse, I want to succeed even as my unexpected elevation heightens the contrast, the great disconnect, between my presentation and my desires. No more seedy side streets now, surely: Detection would go beyond the personal. This is financial pages stuff, isn't it? "Head of Major Firm Caught in Police Raid with Pink Bits Showing." I sit and fiddle with these momentous issues, and yet not an hour goes by when I don't wonder what she is up to, what Nok is doing, whether she sits somewhere in a classroom as I have suggested, or is back where I found her on the cold floor of the Star of Love Bar. I mean, the disconnect is momentous, is it not, chasmic, a fault line of a depth and degree of menace I cannot begin to contemplate?

I have reasons to delay my return to her, perhaps, but under this mound of wholesome activity does there not fester a darker, more oblique layer that no doubt must eventually emerge?

—⊸⊹⊶—

There are some things, even on this wholesome home front, that are difficult to relate. It is not long before it begins to emerge that there are certain matters brought forward from the Henshaw years that are not as they should be. I would be the first to admit that mine is not much of an accountant's mind-set, but you would have expected better records, better accounting of money received and disbursed, systems that were more 'transparent,' to use a modern term. You would have expected, and on this I am resolute, that Arthur Henshaw would make himself more accessible as we attempt to understand the history of things and the procedures that had been followed.

I wish he had been.

I did not know then, as I listened to him insist that things would sort themselves out, that golf was now his chief occupation and not law firm management, and that he had full confidence in me; that he had left his wife and was contemplating a retirement of leisure and license with a woman forty years his junior, someone whom I vaguely remembered when told that she had served as his secretary during his last years at Henshaw & Potter.

"Wouldn't you come in just for a morning?" I remember asking. "This shouldn't take long to sort out with your help."

I could have asked him too, had I known then what I later discovered: "And what of Grace? What of the years of solidity, the daughter and grandchildren who expect you to visit together, to grow old together, to see through what you have started? What of the silver hair and the down pajamas, that elegant Victorian home with its aging trees and patinaed rock wall, the bedtime stories of Peter Rabbit? What of those?"

I asked none of this, of course, not knowing the facts.

"Sorry, Alf," he had replied. "No can do."

—⊛—

The task of disentangling the Henshaw morass, it turns out, is rather more complicated than I have expected. It takes some time, several weeks, maybe months, before I will admit it, even to myself, but it is true that in the final analysis Arthur Henshaw may not have been all I had always imagined. You do not, when you have partners, make decisions about funds, about profits, based on personal predilections. You keep better records, I would say, when you seek reimbursement. My loyalty to Arthur is such that I say nothing much of it, do what I can to sort things out without implicating him unduly, but it would be misleading to say that such discoveries do not change the way I think of my former mentor.

I would not have imagined that one day I would come to believe that Arthur Henshaw's feet were made of clay, but the day does arrive. My sense of loyalty demands that publicly I defend him despite my private misgivings, and the task is not made easier by the constant murmurs of disaffection, the undertone of second-guessing by hotheads whose objective, as far as I can ascertain it, is to turn the firm into an assembly line, a revenue machine of sorts, or worse, to merge it into another and end its discrete existence. Arthur

Henshaw may have been, and I hesitate to say this but it is true, dishonest with his partners, but that does not mean we should allow the firm's half-century-old identity to be swallowed up by some outfit of businessmen from the cities of Denver or Houston.

When I left her I had said I would be back, planned to go back at some point, had counted on it, allowed her to count on it, but now things are so complex, such a challenge, that I lose myself in them. I get home late, begin to miss my evening runs, find myself sitting at my little glass table well into the night with Henshaw & Potter paperwork spread out before me. Occasionally I look up from my work and think of it, of Nok waiting there on my whim, of how it had felt, of the satisfactions of it, but then I look back down again and apply myself to the task at hand. You must differentiate between what is real and what is illusion. I will add that I did the right thing by her. Each month there was a wire to the address she had given me, a short note, some explanation about my competing commitments.

I thought of her, in short, and then directed my thoughts away.

Now I will venture into something that I will freely admit makes no sense, something that I am afraid shows a lapse in judgment so severe I toy with omitting it. In the context of all else, the brown girls in their negligees crouched at one's feet, one must wonder what can be left to make the great Buber, Law Firm Head, cringe? What further fraudulent, deluded conduct is he capable of? Well, I would say, this is of a different magnitude, displays a different kind of weakness. That of — brace yourself — vanity.

We are at Star Date 5725 something in the month of Tishri, I believe, where we are led to doubt our own perceptions, our own experiences, as the paths of our lives split and allow us to choose one fork only, with the other remaining out there forever as some sort of inchoate alternative reality. Remember that episode? I do, quite well.

When I become so oblique, you know it is because I am, even now, after all this, embarrassed.

How, you may ask, could this happen?

We find, those of us managing the firm, that we need to bring in a group of consultants to assist in things, to offer guidance on how to replace the old *ad hoc* systems with others more durable. Heading the team we consider hiring is a woman whose appearance strikes a chord with me. More remarkable, perhaps, is that she seems to return my interest. We sit across the table from each other as her group makes its presentation, and again and again I find my eyes returning to her face and each time she is looking at me steadfastly, without flinching, with the same sort of distraction I must be displaying myself.

She is several years younger than I am, very poised, with carefully brushed hair held in place by a pearled clasp. I glance under the table and see her petite brown shoes, camel hair skirt, shapely legs. She sees me looking and instead of looking away she smiles slightly, twirls a pencil between her fingers, may even show a trace of color. It is all quite hard to believe.

At the end of her group's presentation, she lags behind the others as they file out of our conference room and we end up walking side by side to the elevator.

"Who *are* you?" I ask.

She seems taken aback by my tone as much as by my question. I ask it as if she has just landed from nowhere on the carpet beside me.

"I believe I've just given you a presentation," she says, lightly, smiling. "By the same token I might ask: Who are *you*?"

"You may call me Alfred," I say. "You've Mr. Bubered me enough for one day."

"I shall then, Alfred," she says. "Though I do hope you were listening to what I said."

The rest of the group has walked on ahead, is waiting in the elevator lobby.

"I was trying to," I say. "Not always successfully."

"I know," she says softly. "And you weren't making it any easier for me."

It is hard, I find, not to stand and gape at the elevator as the doors close and the interlude ends. One reads about such interactions, wonders about the veracity of it all, and here it is, Buber himself standing and being handed a business card with a home telephone number hastily scribbled in the margin. It is difficult to remember a time when such an event did not lurk somewhere in the shadows of my imagination. It is even more difficult to process that something of this magnitude has in fact occurred.

Could it be a hoax of some sort, a prank? She has made no effort to cloak her feelings, to deflect, concedes good-naturedly and without any sign of discomfort that she might actually want to see me, Alfred Buber, in some context other than that of nuts and bolts.

As I sit in my office I make all sorts of embellishments on it.

~oooo~

We speak several times on the telephone, she and I, always strictly business, although there is an undercurrent of something else that is difficult to ignore.

"I've sent you a final proposal," she says. "Please let me know if there is anything else at all that you would like from us."

"I will," I say, "most certainly."

I am astute enough, have been long enough in the game, to know that when the judgment must be made as to whether we will hire this group or another, I should step back. But then of course nothing has happened, nothing at all beyond a telephone number scratched on a card. In the end they have made a forceful presentation, their ideas are sound, and I back them.

It is one of the first major decisions of the new management committee, and as such it runs into a fair amount of opposition.

"What can these people add?" one hears murmured. "What we have to do to compete is clear."

Those of us who support the idea prevail, in the end.

"What a challenge this will be," she says, when I call to let her know of our decision. "And so fulfilling on a personal level."

I need to fill in a small detail here. I look her up using various resources, drive by her apartment building, dial her number more than once and listen to the message on her machine. I need to know these things, who knows why I do but I do, and the boundaries between what is reasonable and what is not get lost in a mash of hope and doubt. Though the contract is not set to start for several weeks, each time the telephone at my home rings I answer hoping it might be her and am disappointed when it is not.

It is, in the end, all of it, quite inept, quite adolescent. When the team finally takes residence in the offices to do their surveys and implement their proposals, I find myself living in a world of stolen glances, awkward moments, notes left on chairs. I hear her greeting my secretary and my mind begins to wander, and then she is in my office, in a beige sweater with musical notes on it, a short skirt, and I am tongue-tied, blushing, like a virgin bride, not a gray-headed, if not gray-haired, lawyer.

"Do you have time to fill out a questionnaire?" she might ask and I will reply, of course, for you, anything, name the task, and smile a knowing, sated, infantile smile.

"That's a relief," she says. "We're encountering quite a bit of resistance from some of the other partners. What is it with them?"

So we have what we have, and we have adversaries too. It is all quite comforting. The questionnaire may only have thirty questions, but she remains in my office for over two hours. Even then we talk about almost everything except what's on it: her friends, my house ("You'll have to see it," I say vaguely, suggestively, as if this would be quite in the normal course under some view of things), Salisbury, eventually her brother in the air force, my relative in Golders Green.

"You're so well traveled," she says. "People around here tend to be so insular. I wish I'd had the time and leisure to see as much of the world as you have."

"Indeed," I might say. "Someday, perhaps, you will."

The hotheads would take a dim view of this, of course, this burgeoning, illicit romance of the Buber's.

"Ten thousand miles from the office, I suppose you can do as you please," one or another of them would say, if he knew half as much as he thought he did. "Behind our shingle, on the other hand, and on our dime, well, that's a different story."

One night I wait for her in the basement garage, make plausible small talk as I drive her home, venture a manner of groping, inept contact as we sit in the dark outside her building. So let the chips fall where they do. I don't know what to make of it either, to be candid, not the ethical fix of it—how can one's judgment be unclouded when the recommendations are delivered, as they eventually are, privately, in one's office, by someone who casts longing glances between sentences?—not the juvenile thrill of it, not the quiet betrayal in it.

It's not that I don't think of Nok, realize that I have made a commitment of sorts that I intend to keep, nor that the absurdity of the dilemma isn't evident even to me. To the contrary, I think about her all the time. It's not so much a matter of comparing as it is a constant bewilderment, a mixing of metaphors and of times and places that simply cannot be joined as I join them. I will drive with this new woman, this fresh, intelligent American woman into the countryside to see the foliage, to lunch at an inn, and I will wonder what Nok would say to the panorama that stretches below us, to the little finger sandwiches we will eat, to the wine we will pour into plastic glasses and drink on the banks of a frosty stream. As I talk with one person

I will run the same words past another, a real person too, and wonder at the divide within me that allows, on the one hand, a cascade of dreams, and on the other, that disqualifies her so completely from serious thought.

When it is mealtime at the Star of Love Bar, I imagine, one of the women will walk across the alley to a hole in the wall restaurant and return with steaming plates of rice, a ladling of soup, a mix of vegetables.

(On our left, then, we have a little prostitute, a vendor of cunnilingus to all comers, on our right a vendor of office services in cashmere skirt and pearls, and one about whom I am supposed to be making objective judgments.)

⁂

She is very orderly this woman, this romantic interest of mine (I should give her a name, shouldn't I? I am reticent only because I suffer from this absurd notion, this Edwardian rubbish, that one should not callously bandy about a woman's name even if, in the end, one does not think kindly of her), Karen. From what I see in the office, her lists and schedules, how well-organized she is, it is not a far cry, an inordinate speculation, to imagine that she keeps lists of her own, a register of when she's had her hair cut, when her certificates of deposit become due, what she's thought of the restaurants in which she's eaten. She may keep a diary too—I am fairly sure she is the type who would keep a diary—and I picture it as a meticulous little thing with a cloth cover and a laughable little lock which she takes care to close each evening when she is finished writing.

"You could pop that thing with a cake prod," I will have to tell her. "What is the point of all the locking and unlocking."

"If anyone wants so badly to read what I've written," she will reply, laughing, "they're probably entitled to it."

It will be a triumphant moment, of course, to show her my home, this trophy waiting so long, so carefully burnished, on my little hillock west of the city. I will have to recall the gardener, instruct him to rush about pulling up the weeds I

137

have allowed to grow unfettered, to restore some semblance of symmetry. Creepers will doubtless have scarred some of the stonework but it will all be restored easily enough. We can replace the fallen urn, add gravel where the snowplow has singed the driveway, trim the unruly hedges. Mrs. Savage too can return to her past routines, will relinquish, I should imagine with relief, her responsibility for boiled turnips and broccolini with garlic.

Her little frozen packages will become the stuff of humor.

"Don't you think it's time to throw 'Tuesday' away?" Karen will ask as she examines it. She will try to lift a corner of the wrapper but it will all be frozen solid.

"What is it anyway?"

"Who knows?" I say. "Maybe I'll have it someday."

"Maybe you will," she will say. "She's a nice Mrs. Savage, as Mrs. Savages go, but do you have any idea what's really in there? Did you ever check? It's probably laced with things like lard and oleo."

I have, it is true, allowed a lapse in my regimen of running and careful eating. The press of work has made it inevitable. With Karen I will take steps to restore some semblance of it. She does seem to be, her physique suggests this though she has not made mention of it, the type who places importance on physical fitness. At first, I expect, she will struggle to keep up with me, but before too long she will find her stride, stay apace without difficulty. When we're done (twice around the garden, along the bicycle path, through the town), we will stand in the shower together and plan what we will make for dinner. It will become a ritual, of course, but then most things with Karen, I am observing, are a matter of ritual. It does come to seem, with her, after a while, that there was never another way of doing things.

"You have them quite faked out at Henshaw & Potter, you know," I hear her say. "They all think you're one thing and I know you're quite another. How do you do it?"

I will laugh, shrug, make some self-deprecating remark.

"No, seriously. You are the only interesting man in that whole stupid office of drones and tarts."

"They're not all drones," I will say. "Some are cretins. And they're not all tarts either. Some are demonstrably frigid."

We will laugh, make lewd remarks, single people out, this one, that one, for their idiosyncrasies, the foolish things they have said, the absurd pretense in what hangs on the walls of their offices. We will share the gossip she has gathered along the way, who is having an affair with whom, who has been indiscreet, who is most likely to nurture secrets of the most unspeakable kind.

"You really don't believe you have anything that might be of interest to a woman?" she says finally. "I suppose it's all part of your charm. I'll kill you if ever I find out that it's some sort of Huck Finn routine."

I imagine, buried in a drawer somewhere in her apartment in that quaint building on Beacon Hill, are her own memorabilia, remnants of college, high school even, old letters.

"How come I show you all this stuff and you show me nothing?" she will ask.

"I'm just an old warhorse," I tell her. "I have wounds but no memorabilia."

"I don't believe it," will be her response. "I bet you have a trove somewhere that would take the wind out of a bull."

"Women keep this kind of stuff," I tell her. "Men don't."

"You don't have anything like this?" she says, gesturing at her stash of treasures. "Not even a little black book?"

"Not even a little black book," I will tell her.

───

I write to Nok, still, to an address she says is that of a friend, the same address to which I direct my bank wires. It is base, pidgin, trivial stuff. Oh, I could recount it, of course: I am home again. I am well. I hope you are too. It is a long flight, you know, from your place to mine, as many hours in the air as it is on the train and bus to reach your village. Childish stuff without substance. In later letters—and how many are there? Six? Seven? I do not keep a record of it—I venture further afield, add little anecdotes about the Fall air, my village, the simpler quirks of my housekeeper. I try, believe me, to add something of weight, say how much I enjoyed meeting her, how highly I think of her, even, if you can credit this, why it is I think she touches me in the way she does. These latter attempts, of course, I do not mail. How could I? Even if her English were up to it, and it is not, how do you describe something that is unfathomable even to yourself? There is no rhyme or reason to it at all. I went there seeking one thing, you could easily say, and a flaw within me turned it into another.

Oh, I did wax poetic. How could I not on a dark night when, all alone, something within me emerged to slather my rampant thoughts into poetry, ersatz poetry, pidgin thought. Some of the letters I sent. Others remain in the drawer. Slide it open, my dearest, when you sit at this desk. Here is what you will find among the bits of paper, toffee wrappers, receipts for stays in hotels not a soul in the civilized world knows I have visited.

> *Dear Nok:*
>
> *I wish I spoke your language, or that your English was better. Perhaps the person who translates for you will manage to convey what I am trying to say. What I am trying to say is this. You are the mistress of your body and it is not a personal matter for me what you were doing to make a living when we met. I do not believe that it touches anywhere that is important inside of you. I do not believe that it is unclean.*

It is in the drawer because it was not sent. Here is one that was received:

> *Dear Mr. Alfred:*
>
> *Thank you for letter, and for money which come. I pay woman to read letter for me. Thank you. I not work now. I go school. I wait you come back.*

140

Or this from a night when I must have been feeling particularly poetic, an effusive little fuck if I say so myself, the deluded in pursuit of the baffled.

> *I don't know what love is. I am not sure I ever have known with one possible exception a very long time ago so I can't say what it is that has overtaken me in knowing you. I came to your place pursuing one thing but left having found quite another. I don't believe much in destiny, but I do believe that there are reasons why things happen the way they do.*
>
> *I know the risks of it. Who doesn't? They are of every type. All I can say for sure is that I want to spend time with you and to try and understand you. We are just human beings, you and I.*
>
> *In the end we are both just human beings.*

And from poor bewildered Nok:

> *Mr. Alfred:*
>
> *The money you sent me it is more than enough take care me and my parents too. I am not so hard to understand. I am a girl from a humble place. I want humble things. My dreams are so simple you can laugh at them. I think everything in America too big for me. I think I cannot happy in a place like America.*

Oh, Mr. Alfred. See my dearest how he proposes to respond to this, and then thinks better of it, apparently, and tucks his note back into the drawer.

> *You question whether you would be happy in America. I don't know if it is too big for you or not. What I worry about rather is that daydreams cannot survive the scrutiny of daylight, a winter's day in Boston, snow and slush, you wrapped in layers of clothing and picking your way through puddles of iced water, so very far from home.*

There is a place in a fable called Shangri-La. It is a mountain kingdom where everything is so perfect that no one ever ages. A man like me, a dull and colorless man, falls in love with a beautiful and spirited girl there and wants to take her away with him. The problem is that only in Shangri-La is she young and beautiful. If she leaves she will show her true age, the hundreds of years that life in paradise have kept from her face.

I do not know what the end of this will look like. I do not want to hold out false hope or to harm you. I promise you that.

I will telephone you at the number you have given me.

I missed her. I did. I yearned for her. There is, bluntly, for an aging and pudgy frustrato, the arms and the legs of it, the smoothness of the stomach, the sweetness of the skin, but those desires are transient, emerge and evaporate with predictable mundanity. I would like her here because— why?—because I would, because the thought of it fills me with heat. I could try to put this into words, but how at sea do I want her to be? As it is I imagine her receiving my letters, showing them to others, perhaps to the woman, if it is a woman, whose room she is using. I imagine that if she does not discard them she keeps them in a bureau plastered with Disney stick-ons and on which she keeps a collection of stuffed animals.

(I have overheard a man talking, at the airport the night I left, of a bar girl he had met, how he had fallen for her, after he returned home had responded to her supple little requests for money, not for herself of course, he says laughing, but for sick parents, a dying buffalo back at the village, emergencies of every kind and color, how he had received in return long and loving letters. He had returned to see her and discovered that he had been fooled, that she was a predatory being, after all, that she was receiving support from, sending similar letters to, a dozen men abroad.

"Conniving little bitches, all of them," I overhear him say.)

Her letters arrive and it thrills me when I see them in my little green postbox even though they are uninformative, as flat, as lifeless in their own way, as are mine. She is studying English as I requested she should, thanks me for the money I sent, was sick last week but now she is better. They do not have seasons like the *'Fallen'* I have described to her, she tells me. It is always hot and sticky. She misses me. She wishes I would come back. Do I yet have a date for this? She encloses a picture, believe it or not, one of herself and another she says is her sister standing in front of the Star of Love Bar. I am surprised at how little I remember of her face. I remember more her voice, can almost hear it, as if she were sitting in my car right beside me.

There is a fault line running through all this — do you think I cannot see it? — as thick as a fist and it is only growing, cannot mend.

One evening, after a dinner at Nigel's house, when I have finished bringing him up to date on affairs at Henshaw & Potter, he tells me, quite matter-of-factly, almost incidentally, that there is something I should know. Were it not for his casual manner I would be startled, but as it is I settle back in my chair, cup in hand, prepared to listen.

He has been diagnosed with cancer, he tells me, and won't live much longer.

"What do you mean?" I ask.

He looks perfectly healthy, has just eaten a good meal, listened with interest to what I have been saying, commented on my evolving view — which I have shared with him and no other — of Arthur Henshaw.

"Take it from me," he has said gruffly, smiling, "those Brahmin types are seldom quite what they make themselves out to be."

"What about treatments?' I ask, stunned. "One doesn't just give up."

"You do if you have been told there are no options," he says. "If the cure's worse than the disease."

I am surprised at how hard I take the news, when all is said and done. It is not as if I have not moved on, constructed my own life, left those days spent in Nigel's cramped spare room far behind. As I drive home that evening I feel shaken, riven with sadness, on the edge of weeping. With Nigel gone, reference points will be few and far between.

Dire prognosis aside, he continues to go to work, to function, is still himself.

"These things happen," he says as if discussing a rainstorm or an I.R.S. audit. "We have to take it in stride and deal with things as they are rather than as we wish they would be. I've had a good inning, you know. It's best not to be ungracious."

I am drawn more frequently to the house Nigel shares with his wife, to the place where this great American adventure began and of which I do not have unambiguously pleasant memories. The little room under the stairs that was once mine is quite unchanged, the same books on the bookshelf that were there almost a quarter century before, the bedspread. The single bed looks so small and forlorn each time I pass the door. One evening, after dinner, when his wife has left the room, can be heard pottering about in the kitchen, I am tempted to spill my guts, to try and describe to him my confusion. Rather than these pithy tales of law firm intrigue, these enjoyable chats of Salisbury in the old days, long dead relatives, let me take him on a walk through my recent life, ask for his advice. He is a good person, a sound person, Nigel. He would listen. Let him take my strange saga with him to the grave.

I start equivocally several times, but it seems I can't tell any of it without giving it its entire perspective, and I can't give it perspective without telling everything, and everything stretches so far back, encompasses so much, that it is not, indeed, possible even to begin. Do I mention the dirty rooms? The wet towels on crooked chairs? It is simply not, it is not, as sordid as words would make it seem. But words are words. Wouldn't I, the great scribe Buber, know it better than anyone?

What if he reacted, as he well may, with horror, with disdain, with disgust?

"Oh my God, Alfred. Please say you're not serious."

It is impossible. There is no place in this room, in this house, for a sentence that includes a reference, no matter how oblique, to the Star of Love Bar. I have no vocabulary sufficient to the task. If I had any inclination to be honest with him, it evaporates.

Things remain with Nigel as they have always been: polite, helpful, and aloof.

When Nigel fails the changes are perceptible, obvious, constant. One day he is up and eating at the table, the next he cannot rise from an armchair without assistance, a week later he needs assistance even to walk a short distance.

"Damned thing," he mutters as he creeps across the room. "Damn, damn thing."

His wife tells me that the faculty is holding a tribute to him — Nigel tries to inject humor into what is obviously a sad occasion, calls it "a retirement party without a watch" — and asks if I will attend. The affair is in the ballroom of a suburban hotel. There's a table with food, a cash bar, a little microphone mounted on a podium. At some point the chairman of his department begins proceedings, recounts Nigel's tenure, his contributions, and then others mount the podium and pay tribute. They have written poems, ditties, make speeches that show genuine warmth. All along Nigel stands to the side with his wife and takes it in with characteristic stoicism. For a moment it is as if he were simply going on some particularly arduous journey, a train ride where he must remain incommunicado, and is taking with him the crowd's good wishes as if that will somehow make it all more purposeful. I listen, both admiring and a little envious of how warmly he is regarded, how much effort people have made to be pithy and insightful in their offerings, but there is also a sense of how trivial it all is, all the minding, the good conduct, the careful choices.

145

I am no nihilist, believe me, but one way or another, win, lose or draw, it does come down to this, a crusty farewell, and all is done.

⁜

I find myself spending a great deal of time with Nigel now. He is in and out of the hospital, linked to all manner of tubes and drains, becoming palpably weaker each time I see him. More than once I am tempted again to talk freely to him, to show him an awkward and twisted gratitude by being honest, but the opening is never there. Eventually he is too far gone and I find myself instead doing the equally unimaginable, stroking his hand, combing his hair, feeding him chocolate piece by piece. Hours pass this way.

I have other, mounting, commitments of course, but it is the least I can do.

"Thank you, Alfred," he says and then he gasps: "Life is very short, you know."

Would it be ungracious to give voice here to something that a little voice keeps saying within me even as I sit by his bedside, hold a glass to his lips, look up anxiously each time a juvenile-looking doctor comes in, sassy and bright with his stethoscope and charts to tell us nothing new? Is this an opportune time to note that, though I cannot shake the feeling of grief and loss, neither can I lose the edge of relief that creeps upon me and that is a constant companion to sadness in the gloomy hospital room? With his death imminent an internal meter will at long last be switched off, a reminder of how things might have been otherwise, of other aspirations, other courses, other possibilities.

One critic, at least, will have been permanently silenced. The other will turn to ashes only when I do.

⁜

Such busy times, such comings and goings, at Henshaw & Potter. The consultants scurry about the corridors. There are constant meetings. It all acquires a life of its own. The pace of things quickens to a point where I wonder whether a semblance of normality will ever return.

Destiny has several objectives of its own, several little tests, apparently, that my behavior in past lives mandates I confront in this one. A secretary taps my shoulder in the middle of a meeting to tell me that I am urgently needed on the telephone. I walk briskly to my car, drive to the hospital, and there Nigel's wife awaits me as if I have brought with me some answers, some solution. Nigel's destiny I suppose was that his disease would kill him slowly, take him in pieces so that on the afternoon he died, a bright spring afternoon it was, there would be nothing much of him left, a gasping husk on a bed with his wife on one side of it and me on the other. It seemed too much to contemplate at that moment that it should all simply end like that, with a whisper and a twitch. The room fell suddenly silent and there we were, his wife and I, each of us holding a lifeless hand.

"I'm so sorry," I say. "I owe a great deal to him."

"He thought of you as a son," his wife says, and strangely enough it had come to feel as if we were somehow more closely bound than we had always seemed. I had thought that with his death I would gain at least freedom from his constant and silent criticism, but instead a feeling of loneliness descends and it offers nothing in the way of solace or freedom. I am named executor in his will and find myself responsible for the practical aspects of his estate. He was not a wealthy man by any measure, an academic of sorts, author of a textbook, investor in several very ordinary mutual funds, but nevertheless it is yet another distraction.

"What would I have done without you?" his wife asks.

I don't mean to be churlish about this, I do it gladly enough, but time does pass, the months do go by, the more tasks I seem to complete the more new tasks I seem to acquire. But of my churlishness there is no question. At times I hardly recognize the snorting bear that stamps inside of me.

 ⸻

147

One night, late, following what instinct I cannot say, I call overseas directory assistance and ask them if they have a number for the Star of Love Bar. All manner of frittering about ensues as the operator fusses with an echoing slate of foreign-sounding voices.

I *kibbitz*, spell the words several times, may begin to sound brusque.

"Is this a business?" the woman asks. "Do you mean a bar, in the sense we understand it? A bar?"

"Yes," I say.

"Are you sure this bar is still there?" a faint voice from faraway asks.

"Yes," I say. "It is really there."

They do find it, in the end, reel off a series of numbers, ask if I want to be connected. No, I say. I'll call myself sometime later when it is more convenient. The phone, as I recall, is on the counter across from the door. It is morning there, but the Star of Love Bar is open. I wonder if there are customers yet.

"Nok boyfriend," Pla will explain. "He call from America."

Maybe an early customer, his hand cupping the head of a girl, will look up from the bench. Maybe he will manage a smile. Who knows? It has been months since I left her. It is all becoming quite remote. Is that then how it is destined to end, simply to fade away, to become little more than a set of quirky, tangled images?

—————

Apparently not.

It seems that I am destined, in my middle years, to experience all sorts of things for which I am not prepared. My path, or so it would appear, not only takes me to the East where I am to leave a tugging part of myself, to plant the seed, so to speak, of my life's unmooring; not only includes my accession to Henshaw's elevated post within the firm, and an unexpectedly wrenching bereavement; but now I am to witness the unraveling of my professional life, of my reputation, and to do so stoically and without complaint. I am expected, or so I am led to believe, to immolate myself, and then to express gratitude for it.

I know that times change, that ways of doing things that once made sense may not be appropriate forever. On the other hand, I can't see what it is the hotheads are after. I stand in their way, yes, but these are honest differences, or so I had thought. They would have us move from our quarters, spend millions of dollars on all sorts of new technologies, employ a variety of expensive technocrats to change the entire fabric of Henshaw & Potter, and I have opposed them. I knew they bridled at my obstruction, but I did not know the lengths to which they would go to prove their point.

How else to explain that, on a Friday afternoon while I am sitting at my desk taking care of some matter or other, I am visited by a delegation of stern-faced young men and women who inform me, stiffly but with what may pass for courtesy, that they have a matter of the utmost gravity they need to discuss with me. I gesture to the several chairs in my office, invite them to seat themselves, indicate that I am listening. They are so uneasy, this band of upstarts, have so clearly caucused and caucused this visit, that the tension mounts even as they shuffle about, exchange looks, steal glances at me that smack of both empathy and impudence.

"Have you come to execute me?" I ask, attempting to infuse the proceedings with a modicum of levity. "Your faces suggest it."

No, a serious, businesslike young woman says, not that, though what they have to say is as serious as could be.

"Go ahead then," I say, and I smile, rest my chin on the backs of my clasped hands.

"It concerns the consulting firm that was recently hired," I hear, and of course at once I believe I understand what this is all about, why their discomfort is laced with antagonism.

"What of it?" I say. "My feeling is that they are doing exactly what they were retained to do."

"Well, it's not that," I am told, and now I am being regarded sternly by this brace of mercenary young people, their discomfort replaced by something that appears to resemble anger.

"You've lost me," I say, and from the looks I now get, this barrage of righteous glances, I realize, suddenly, that I am about to be surprised.

"We have received a complaint," I hear, "of harassment. It has been lodged by one of their key employees, a woman. The complaint is fairly explicit in its description of actions by you that would be completely inappropriate if true."

"Do you know something?" I say, becoming annoyed. "I haven't the faintest idea what you're talking about."

One of the more level-headed of the delegation, a young man I have in fact had a hand in training, now speaks up and his manner is, if not conciliatory, at least less strident.

"She says, Alfred," he begins, "that since the first day she started here your behavior towards her has been, well, inappropriate."

I interrupt him.

"You're talking about Karen W.," I say.

(I omit the last name here. Buber, when all else is said and done, cannot bring himself to spell it out, to vomit it out, to iden-tify her in this obscene dialog.)

"Yes," I am told. "It is she who has made these allegations."

"If you'd care to," I say, becoming acidic, "perhaps you'd tell me what it is I'm supposed to have done."

"She says you've followed her home," the boy says. "Parked outside her house and watched her windows. She says she has pictures of you there. That you repeatedly make suggestive remarks, that you brush against her."

He pauses, shakes his head.

"Hell, Alfred. Don't force us to be more graphic. This is lawsuit material. You can't do this sort of thing in this day and age."

The room echoes now with the moments of silence that ensue. I remain in my seat, my old office now an alien place filled with chilly air and hostile objects. The fabric in my clothes prickles. My face burns. If I had thought I had fully immersed myself in the art of bereavement at Nigel's death, this is a moment far more profound, far more searing than that. The faces, the angry, burning little eyes, the postures, the suits, all bear down like meteors set to ignite.

"This is a miserable task," someone says. "We are sorry."

"Then why are you doing it?" I ask frostily.

No one answers, I suppose no one could answer, and there is a further stretch of silence. I know what they are waiting for, what they are hoping I will say, but I deny it them. I need to leave, to go back to my house on the hill, to sit on a chair somewhere and to take stock. I need to add up what it is I have in life and what it is I do not have, and then I need to see what I think, to understand what I need.

"Is that it, then?" I ask, and stand.

We're not sure, I am told. In this day and age allegations such as this cannot be put aside without some measure of remedy.

—⊗⊗⊗—

Mrs. Savage's food is bland but nutritious. It is indeed, on those evenings when she does not stay late, kept in labeled packages so that all I need do is unwrap them and place what she has made on a plate. When that is done, I carry the plate into my white room and eat at the round table I have set in its center. On some evenings I read while I eat, on others I sit quietly and watch the goings on in the garden as the light fades and the birds sweep about preparing for darkness.

CHAPTER SIX

I Buber on. What choice do I have?

Oh it is distasteful; of course it is distasteful to struggle down a passage past a thousand desks each morning. I pass secretaries, clerks, lawyers, and it is in their eyes, each of them, a prurient mix of sympathy and of curiosity, a brew of judgment, all of it ill-informed and ugly. A sense of instability pervades things too, would even without the abrupt departure of the consultants, not just the one group but all of them, the sudden quiet that settles over the whole of Henshaw & Potter. Supposedly I continue to head the firm, but these things, scurrilous rumors of this nature, are the fodder of places such as ours. Things cannot last. I see that.

We meet, the management committee, but it is clear to me that we are a tired-looking group, dinosaurs really, men in withered suits and with starchy manners, computer illiterates, polite beyond reason, completely obsolete. Ranged against us is the firm's heartbeat, a group that imagines itself imaginative with youth and daring and in all likelihood, if push comes to shove, clients on their side. They have not yet made their move, but they will. I suppose I could have been, at one time, conciliatory, thrown in my lot with them, but in the long run what would that have achieved? Change for change's sake has never appealed to me. You have to be true to yourself.

On the other hand, Arthur Henshaw's legacy, or so it turns out, whatever that legacy may be, is itself hardly worth preserving.

"This is all so crass," one of the dinosaurs mutters.

"These are crass times," I say.

There is no mention, at least in this group, of that other matter, that supposedly great indiscretion for which I am supposedly due an eternity in the hellfire of uncertainty, insurance consultation and analysis.

("The youngsters just wanted to bring you down a notch or two," one old fool tells me. "It'll pass. In the old days . . ."

Bring me down a notch or two! Bring me down a notch or two! Is that even possible?)

A young chap, one of the brightest of them, announces that he is leaving for another firm and we find out, of course, that several others will be following suit, a group of major clients in tow. It has always been inevitable, but now there are all sorts of hurried phone calls to the firm's clients, reassurances, a hasty rearrangement of resources, but it is like stemming a tide with hand towels. Those lawyers who creep into my office to pledge their loyalty to the old firm are — it is lost on no one — the halt and the lame, those with nowhere else to go. Times change, they do, and it occurs to me that I am already descending into the state of my greatest dread, experiencing a kind of vulnerability I last felt when I stepped off the plane from Salisbury. Except that this time I lack the defense I had then, even if I did not then know it: of the future, that things would be better in the future.

It drags on, but it is fairly clear that Henshaw & Potter, if it survives at all, will be a quite different institution. Several of my colleagues decide to retire and the dinosaurs, their numbers thinning, find themselves balanced on the razor edge of the remaining hotheads' pleasure. Some old coot comes doddering into my office with the suggestion that we found a new firm ourselves, start over, but I see myself leading a pack of the feeble, have no energy for it. I am not a wealthy man, relatively speaking, but if I trim my spending, abandon my fortress, I could retire myself, survive.

So it is, for now, that I traipse in each morning, plod to the cafeteria at lunchtime, leave on the dot at five. Law firm, Mercedes, garage, running clothes, bike path, white room, bookstore, bed. The sun rises, it is all repeated. There is a truce of sorts at Henshaw & Potter, a delicate affair in which the two camps are scrupulously polite with each other, but continue to size things up, remain vigilant.

Fine. I complete my daily circle, move papers about on my desk, confer with my secretary. One way or another there is no retreat possible now, or not yet, and so we all soldier on, the old guard, with empty offices, quiet corridors, a constant reproach. There is nothing more you can do, is there, nothing more you can do to prepare, no home however lavish, no bank account however full, that you can step into to fill the void when the simple fact of it is that you are not wanted where you are.

I have to admit, now that it is upon me, that what I most dread may also be what I most want. What I have is solitude, unconnectedness, a Spartan kind of penury.

—∞∞∞—

How ironic is it—well, I suppose it's all ironic in a way— that as I walk through the street I hear my name called, once, twice, see a young woman carrying a child hurrying towards me.

"Alfie?" she says. "It is. It's Alfie."

I'm wary. Oh I'm wary. Everything these days where attractive young women of the species are concerned is enough to make me wary.

"You don't recognize me do you?' she says. "I must say I barely recognized you, but it's you."

I look at her carefully and then it dawns on me, it dawns on me with a disappointing, unnerving clarity, who it is I am looking at.

"Rebecca," I say. "Good heavens. It is."

With the baby somehow tucked under her arm she reaches out and hugs me, and even after all this time there is something familiar in it, in the solidity of her frame, the leaden smell of her hair.

"You look good," she says, holding me at arm's length.

"I'm an old bloody man," I say. "It's you who looks good. You look very good. Very sound."

"Old?" she says. "What are you? An antique. Forty-two? Forty-three? On the other hand, you were old even then, back in that horrible rooming house."

"And a baby?" I say. "Is it yours or did you steal it?"

She laughs, an easy, throaty laugh, familiar too except that something about her is different. The coarseness is gone, the air of disorder. She is wearing a brown woolen dress, an elaborate beaded necklace, long earrings. Her hair, once a mess of curls and dreadlocks, is loosely wound and clipped at the back. She has become beautiful.

"I stole it," she says.

She tells me that she is married, has been for several years, and relatively happily too. She is a web designer, she tells me, her husband a baker, someone she met (and here she slaps my arm: "You'd get this," she says) when she was still drawing fruit and pastries for grocery store promotions.

"It's okay," she says. "It turned out okay. And you?"

She has me on a bad day, of course, but for whatever reason I do not want her to know. I cannot, today least of all, allow that.

"I'm still a lawyer," I say instead.

"Don't tell me you're still at that same place, Higgle-shack and Bottom or whatever?" she says.

"Henshaw & Potter," I say with a tired smile.

"Yeah," she says. "That's it. I knew it was a name with something wrong in it. I can't believe you're still there. You hated it."

"I did?" I say. "I don't remember telling you I hated it."

"Are you kidding," she says, shifting the child from one arm to the other. "It always sounded to me like they abused the heck out of you. It's all you used to talk about, that and how the jerk who owned the place, Higgleshack whatever, used to torture you. I always wondered why you didn't just tell him to go fuck himself. You must have wanted to every day. Remember that time he walked into your office on a Friday night and told you to do something by Monday, and you worked all weekend? And it turned out the customer called the thing off on Friday evening and he forgot to tell you."

"I don't remember that," I say.

"I can't believe you're still there," she says.

We talk for a while longer. The infant begins to squirm. How much can you say about designing graphics for computer screens? We exchange telephone numbers—she is living in Portland, Maine, in an old farmhouse which she and her husband are restoring on weekends—but it is obvious that neither of us has the intention of actually calling.

"I remember," she says as we part, "that you used to talk about building a house, and that's where I first got the idea. Come and see what we've done. I mean it. You'll like my husband. He's a really good guy."

"I will," I say, though of course it is the last thing on earth that I will ever do.

———∞———

It seems then that everyone, or almost everyone, has the potential for reformation, for redemption, and that somewhere there must be the path that I am destined, one way or another, to find, to trip into, to take. It is ironic, as I say, that I should run into Rebecca because in the light of all else that has happened, Nigel's death, Henshaw's trail of deceits, the chaos in my livelihood, it is my running into Rebecca that has the most profound impact on me, that decides for me what it is I need to do.

I have allowed my bank wires to Nok to expire so that several months have now gone by without any word from me to her, anything from her to me. I have all but resigned myself to the belief that Nok is little more than a mirage, that I have drained the essence of this affair so that there is nothing left of it but sediment. What has it been, after all, from the start, but a few squalid moments, a few days in the heat of the summer? The basic predicates of a substantive exchange are lacking, have always been lacking. Its end has always been just a matter of time . . .

I could try to reach her by telephone, I suppose, by calling the Star of Love Bar, just to check in, just to check. I will ask how her English classes are going, if she has stayed the course, hear news of the young women who surround her, of Pla, of her parents up on their platform in the mountains. But I am at a crossroads now and the point is that either I am to board a plane and go back, make good on my promise, to find out if it is even possible to make good on my promise, or it is time to let this end, let the whole thing go, once and for all.

It is a logical choice, and it is one I have no choice but to make. Events themselves, or so it would seem, have led me to this like a dog forced to put his nose in a puddle of urine. I have allowed things of no consequence, matters of no lasting weight, to place their fists on the scale of things, to keep me from doing, honestly and forthrightly, the one thing that I have wanted to do, rightly or wrongly, sinfully or not sinfully, sacredly or in profanity, the one thing that has ever shown promise of breaking the bonds that have held me for too long. Now that they have fallen aside one by one, I will welcome my courtship with catastrophe, if it is catastrophe that awaits me. Maybe what awaits will clear away the smog and the filth that has come to cloud whatever it is that is my destiny.

To hell then with the village store owners, what they may think, say behind their hands. To hell with the board of aldermen and its petty concerns, the stalagmites at Henshaw & Potter and their fossilized prejudices. I am blind half the time, or so it would seem, except to imagined insults, the judgments of others about whom I care not one whit. What is Nok to them? What are my failings to them? What is it all but one massive titter over dinner? There are risks to change now. All sorts of risks.

They are not the risks that should keep me in the throes of a living *rigor mortis*.

The thought of Nok in Boston is one that thrills and at the same time one that the imagination can barely contain. She will know—soon she will know—what it means to drive in a big dark Mercedes-Benz. She will know, as I open the door for her and she inhales the rich leather, sees the shining walnut on the dashboard, the car telephone, the blinking alarm light, that she is in way over her head, that unless I am careful she will drown, simply submerge and never come up again. She will sit beside me, small and with newfound grace, as I start the engine and we begin to move. She will look around, watch the kid leather gloves I wear as I turn the wheel, pay the attendant, join the stream of traffic back into the city. We will both be in awe, she of the power, me of the blackness of the road.

But then she is, is she not, a person after all, a real human being, far more than an open mouth crouched on a stone floor, the figment of some fantasy? She is a person with intellect and potential, likes and dislikes, a history all her own. Her father was once a policeman, she has said, wounded in the line of duty, but not so badly that he could not work if he truly wanted to. He receives a pension, she says, but not an adequate one, loafs about on the platform, keeps a few chickens and ducks in a coop under the house, but does not care for them. Her parents married when they were very young, her mother fourteen, and she suspects her father has had a series of affairs his whole life.

"When he young," she has said, over a bowl of fried rice, "he handsome. Now he old and ugly."

And she has been to school, of course, every day in a white shirt and long skirt until it became too expensive and she followed the path of so many others.

"What kind of school?" Buber has pressed, this Buber anxious to bring this girl to terms he can grasp. "What did it look like? Where was it? Did I see it when I was there?"

It was just a school, she insists, a school like all others, a building several miles from the village with a starting bell, a headmaster, detentions, wooden desks. But no, Buber needs to know more: Did the unspoken secret extend into that little schoolhouse, an uneasy feeling make its way into the consciousness of the pretty girls as they sat squirming at their desks, that for them there may lie ahead this consorting with foreigners in the city, this flirting with shame as a last refuge from poverty?

(What is it, you paunchy foreigner, that you want? Take off her clothes and smother her in whatever it is you want except your mindless curiosity, your aimless intrusions that seek to go beyond disrobing and into a part of her that she never agreed to disclose to you. What you want to do, Buber, is to strip her truly naked, more naked than any foreigner who has come before you has ever managed to do, to expose things never before exposed. Then, deep down you know, you will truly have had her.

Then, deep down, you know you will leave and she will not be any the better for it.)

It was a school like all others, she insists. How exotic, for heaven's sake, how unhuman, do you think I am?

I do not know how long I will be gone. Mrs. Savage will come each day and make sure that things are in order. The most valuable of my possessions are secured in a lockbox. The bank will pay my bills. I tell the hotheads that I need time to think things over, that they can have the firm and the clients that were never really mine after all, that all I require is an office and the stipend that they are obligated to pay me in any event. They readily agree, are quite generous, in fact, in their accommodations.

From the depths of my medicine cabinet I begin the process of reassembling my pharmacy, the balms and disinfectants and soaps and sprays, brush off the canvas pouch and money belt, the bush jacket with its collection of pockets and zippers. An old feeling, anticipation of the sort one feels only as a child, begins to well within me. I approach the airlines, make my calls, begin to plan this whole thing in my head.

And so the day approaches. I close the door of my house, drop the key off with a realtor who has undertaken to respond to any emergencies, and drive my car to the garage where it will be stored.

It feels like jumping from a cliff and exhaling, all at once.

And then, of course (but you have been expecting this), from out of the blue, on the eve of my departure, a Saturday, looking out the window of my great monastery, I see a taxicab draw up, turn a slow circle on the gravel I have so carefully planned for the expanse before the portico. Normally the gravel makes its own distinctive crunching as tires pass over it, but on this morning, a frozen winter morning that is cold and dry and without even a fleck of snow on the ground, with the brown leaves of autumn scattered about and frozen in place like rotting pieces of wrapper, the car approaches in complete silence. It is yellow, one of the lights on its roof is broken. I see through the windscreen that the driver wears a plaid cap. In the back seat is a young woman.

How to describe the moment?

I stand at the window and wonder what this is all about. There are taxis in this town, though not many, and I can count on the fingers of one hand the occasions they have had to make their way up my drive. The door opens and the woman steps out. I would have said she was about twenty years old. (I am off by three years, but how could I have expertise in such things?) She has long dark hair and a trim physique, wears a camel hair coat, brown slacks, suede boots. She carries a small bag over her shoulder, makes her way to my front door and rings the bell as the taxi waits.

There would have been a time, need I say it, when such an event would have piqued my curiosity, more than that, would have snapped me loose in an instant from the mooring to which my thinking was always so closely tethered. Not so this morning. In a matter of hours I was to leave. My thoughts were elsewhere as I opened the door in response to her ring.

Let me pick from moments that follow to describe what I saw. She is tall and really quite beautiful, lovely, is lovely, surpassingly lovely. Her best features are her nose and her mouth, the former almost fragile in how perfect it seems despite that it is not perfect, has a little bump, a small bump, just below the bridge. Her mouth is, in fact, perfect, and moves easily into a smile that reveals flawless teeth. I have of course now seen — she had in her wallet, indeed — a recent picture of her mother. In middle age Veronica has lost what hints there once may have been of beauty. Her smooth complexion and startling cheekbones have shifted into an angularity that has turned her quite harsh. While Alice does resemble her in some ways — thick dark hair, sallow skin — one would be hard pressed to discern her ethnicity. Her mother's doll-like affectation has become bird-like in middle age, while Alice is graceful and willowy.

"May I help you?" I remember saying as I opened the door, took in the taxi man watching from beside his car.

"Alfred Buber?' she asked.

"Yes," I replied cautiously.

"My name is Alice Wang," she said, and as she said this something extremely strange happened to me, the blood rose to my face, my heart began to rush, the afternoon lightened until everything around the girl appeared quite white.

"Veronica's daughter?" I said softly, scrutinizing her face with its startling resemblance to my mother's, as if pictures of my mother in her youth had been touched by an Asian magician eager to transform her.

She launched then into an apology, she should have written, called perhaps, but she had found herself unable to do either, could only picture herself standing on my doorstep just as she indeed then was, even with the taxi idling in the background. She had found me, she said, by ransacking the alumni office at the law school (or at least so she put it), scouring a legal directory, pestering the switchboard at Henshaw & Potter. In the end it had not been that difficult. I am not, after all, for all the things that I am, elusive.

"I hope you aren't angry," she said.

"Not angry," I said. "Not at all."

There was a moment of silence then, a heavy, fraught moment during which we examined each other unabashedly, searched for all manner of things we ourselves could not have identified.

"In fact," I believe I added, "I think I'm delighted."

She smiled, appeared to relax, and together we gestured to the taxi man that he could leave, that I would take care of getting her where she later needed to be. For all the pleasure I felt, indeed, there was a moment in which the customary awkwardness of things intruded. I extended my arms to her and she did not come forward, lingered instead and then stepped closer, even that gesture perhaps only to avoid embarrassing me. I placed my hands on the back of her coat, the felty back of her coat, caught the sweet grassiness of my daughter's hair. She had no sheltering pretext. This trip to find me was a graduation present from her grandfather. She was staying at a hotel in Cambridge. She would be starting at Stanford Law School shortly.

All this in the first minute. We were still on the doorstep, mind you, and now I hustled her in, closed the door, took her coat. Her eyes wandered up the walls, out onto the lawns, along the portico, but I took her elbow and guided her into the great room. She wanted nothing from me, she then said, nothing at all beyond this, just to be in the same room with me.

"I know that," I said.

We then, as I recall it, began a conversation consisting of profound sentiment interlaced with banalities almost as profound.

My house, you will find, for all it does offer, is very low in technology. There is no DSL line, whatever that may be, though I do have a computer and if you choose to plug it into the telephone, somehow you can find your way onto the internet. I will confess I have not done it since I was shown how by some boy who came out with the equipment and assured me it would work better with this special cable of his, but I assume it all works. You will find an alarm system that may qualify for antique status, a single television set in the bedroom, a series of rotary telephones. I do have access to cable television and there are dozens of program choices. I tend to watch older programs, the ones that require no thinking and yet pass themselves off as original, the ones where the colors seem to be faded and the people themselves dated and clumsy. On some nights I watch until a glow appears around the curtains at the window.

Your mother did make a point of her father's wealth in the old days. (I speak as if I really knew her. I did not. You will have gathered that. I am sure she has many virtues, ironic though you were when you spoke of her. She does have, does she not, a tendency to fixate on small things, something that suggests to me you are right when you laughingly referred to her ability to conduct vendettas that run forever, including hers against me.) Your schooling in Switzerland and education at Stanford, among other things, suggest that my relative wealth will not change much for you. But it is yours, all of it, without restriction.

My business affairs will not be difficult to learn. Do not feel that you intrude, please do not, when you sit at my desk. I hereby invite it, welcome it. There are shares, bonds, almost a half-a-million dollars in a checking account. The house has no mortgage. Sell it if you care to or keep it as a curiosity. It will be worth something to the right buyer, though more than one real estate broker has raised his eyebrows at me on discovering that the landmark on this mound is mine—conceived, designed, executed by me. My stockbroker's name and number is in the desk. He will inform you on such arcane matters as the basis in my shares, capital gains taxes owed, mutual fund performances. The reality of it is that I have not paid much attention to matters such as this. At the height of my law career, it was often a chore deciding how to place what remained of my income once my own needs were met.

My old law firm, Henshaw & Potter, are my lawyers. You may find something about the firm, something in the atmosphere when you visit, that unsettles you. At some point you may decide to cut all ties with Henshaw & Potter. I would have no objection to that. Go through everything. Open drawers at will.

Here. I will do it for you.

> *Dear Mr. Buber: Many thanks for your generous contribution to the Republican National Committee. We would be honored if you would attend . . ."*

> *Dear Mr. Buber: We acknowledge with gratitude your generous gift to the Simon Wiesenthal Foundation . . ."*

> *Dear Mr. Buber: We have received your generous donation to the Holocaust Museum Foundation . . .*

I pull these out with something approaching humor, not to make a point of my generosity (the donations were a pittance, truthfully), but rather to give you a glimpse of the kind of thing you will come across.

This too, I am afraid. (I am tempted as I write to dash about destroying the things that startle even me as I unearth them, but I seem to have lost my sensibilities in a conflagration greater than I am. I will destroy nothing.)

> *White Man, forties, seeks a Woman of any color and religion, aged thirty to fifty, for friendship and possibly more. Must be generous of spirit, flexible of opinion, and respectful of herself and others. A photograph would be helpful.*

My memory is that I toyed with this last, but did not in fact act on it. I cannot then explain the envelope with the photograph of a woman that is clipped to it. I simply do not remember. The woman, looking at her now, appears somewhat sad, looks perhaps overweight, even unkempt. Be that as it may. You will find somewhere too a smattering of pornography, grainy, amateurish stuff that would be, to most people, more of historic than of erotic import. (No toned bodies, exaggerated mouths, dubbed sounds.) Watch the girls' faces carefully, as I did. They appear not to be acting, show no emotion, perhaps at moments an edge of pleasure but nothing more, some embarrassment when it is over. There is nothing vile in it. Things are what they are. A body's urges are what they are.

You will see that I do not have many clothes; four or five jerseys, three pairs of shoes, a dozen shirts in all. You may wonder about this. It has to do with my experience in America, this quirk of mine. I do not care for the looseness, the lewdness, the consume and devour and discard nature of my adopted culture. I keep my clothes, take pride in their wear and their patches, will not consider the notion of using up and replenishing and replacing. Everything, as I see it, is a layer on which another can be built. One does not start constantly afresh.

You will perhaps find if you care to, and when you are done with these notebooks perhaps you will look specifically, evidence of a monthly draft sent for a period of time to a young woman on the other side of the world. When I told you that I was leaving to reunite with a woman I had come to love, that I may well bring her back to my home and marry her, I omitted some details. I dissembled, I'm afraid, when you said, just as you left, how pleased you were that I had found someone.

But then you will doubtless have read all about it in the newspapers by the time you read this. I was a different man that afternoon than I became just one week later.

—∞∞∞—

I cannot sit down now and recite piece by piece the sequence of our conversation. We sat on chairs on either side of an unlit fire and I listened, and she listened, and I learned more in that short window of time than I had ever learned from one person before. Perhaps she was right that there is something genetic in it, a genetic recognition so that as we sat there our bodies recognized each other, the slight curl in her hair, somewhat like that in my mother's, my father's elegant fingers, the inflection in her voice when she asked a question, reminiscent of something I have been surprised to hear in myself on recordings and in those videotapes we once made to train young lawyers. There were things I did not tell her, of course. I expect there were things she did not tell me.

She is a mature girl, this is easy to see, meticulously groomed, beautifully dressed. I try to remember how Veronica once looked, to imagine her standing beside an aging Veronica, Veronica festooned in a designer outfit trimmed with a scarf, a hat, elaborate pointed shoes. It is difficult to believe, after all these years, that I am, after all, still tied to her, that our salad of genes has mingled in this girl. I tried not to ask questions about her mother, but I was curious. For years she had meant nothing to me, had been simply an ambiguous memory. Suddenly she had acquired importance.

"People underestimate my mother," Alice had said. "But there is a logic to how she thinks."

There were bursts of discussion, a dozen topics covered seemingly at once and then, inexplicably for two people with a lifetime of catching up to do, we found ourselves sitting in silence, suddenly at a loss that seemed insurmountable. After a minute or so of it, she looking into her teacup, me I don't know where, I offered to show her my house. We took off down the hall and walked through my quiet rooms, and to break the silence, to say something, I tried to explain what it was I had sought to accomplish with my sudden alcoves and eccentric walls of glass. She took it all in, it seemed, respectful, noncommittal, an unremittingly soft and pleasant presence.

So we walked through the glass atrium and along the colonnade and I was pleased when we encountered a flock of birds, perhaps on their way south, alighting on the white balustrades of the patio. My house is, may be considered, a work of art, or at least I see it as such, especially on moody afternoons when the light hits things in a certain way and the floors gleam and the art stands starkly against the walls.

—⁂—

It is when we return to the great room, back to the gilt chairs facing the fireplace in which we had been sitting, tea-cups on a table between the chairs, that she makes clear to me that she is not just a lost girl, not just a found daughter, that she is more.

She takes her cup from the table, swirls the cold tea about in it, declines more, lapses into a palpable silence.

"Are you okay?" I ask, becoming concerned.

"Yes," she says.

"I hope you're not disappointed or distressed," I say, and she answers quickly that she is not.

"It's just this," she says, and then there is silence again, a quiet that I think best to let pass, to let time itself absorb. "It's just this," she repeats, softly. "You seem so lonely."

I look over and she raises her eyes, fastens them on my face, and to my dismay I see that they are filling with tears.

"I'm sorry," she adds quickly.

Her slender fingers encircle the cup. Her nails are impeccably manicured. The stone in her delicate ring shines. The tears take me aback.

"My dear," I say. "There is no reason for grief. I am perfectly happy, more so for having been visited by you."

Her look is constant, steady.

"I know nothing, you know," she says. "Whenever the subject of my origins came up, they shoved it off quite roughly, but sometimes you—or what I imagined you were—was all I could think about. It's shocking now to see you because you are—pardon me, Alfred, pardon me—as preserved, as apart, as *waiting*, as in my dreams. How could this be?"

"I don't know," I say. "Perhaps there is more to life than we see."

"My relatives in Kowloon are all so delicate and small and there I was, a western giantess, going to an English private school, a fish out of water. But I knew that someday I would find you and that you would understand."

"I will try," I say.

"I also dreamed you'd be tall and handsome," she says and then, as I am on the verge of saying something, disclaiming, apologizing, she adds, eyes down: "But I didn't dream you'd be so elegant, so handsome. I didn't dream you'd be so *beautiful*."

"Well, I don't know about that," I gurgle, embarrassed. One could have pushed me over then with a finger, pulled my lungs from my body with a feather.

I remember the look on her face, the impassive look on her face.

———✺———

After she leaves I unplug the appliances, lock the windows, and walk again through my changed house. The curtains, slightly faded by the sun, are drawn, and the floors give off a deep glow in the filtered light. Staves of afternoon sun press around the edges of the shades and flash across the rugs and the arms of chairs. Jade urns, richly veined, stand on pedestals in the corners. An ivory elephant rests on its teak base at the center of a table. My desk is empty. My house is empty, eerily so.

This, then, is how I left my life as I knew it, took off with not a soul in the world aware of where I was going, or why, not a soul keeping track of me; and though I did not know it at that moment, these empty spaces were all I could think of when, miles away, in the deepest of distress, I remembered how it once was to be safe. As I closed the door I thought of Alice, and a sense of optimism descended on me unlike any I have known.

She is an elegant girl, my elegant girl, tall and groomed and articulate and quick. She has the face of a student, but she carries herself with the grace of someone much older. She moves in a purposeful way, takes long steps, looks completely wholesome.

Nothing that has happened changes any of that.

CHAPTER SEVEN

Outside nothing has changed; the same rumbles, the same odors, the same voices even. I am tired from the long flight, the glimmerings of anxiety, the sense that I am off in orbit, going towards nothing and with nothing to fall back on. There is something unhinged in this, an adventure that writes itself as it goes.

I tell someone on the plane that I am on my way to meet up with my fiancée.

"Local girl, is she?" he has asked.

"No," Buber the Magnificent lies. "An American. She's with the consulate there."

What the fuck? I ask myself. *What the fuck?*

"I thought we had an embassy there," he'd corrected.

"Whatever," I said with a measure of distaste. "She deals with visas and the like, as I understand it."

"Interesting place," he had said. "I go there quite often myself."

The taxi hurtles along the expressway to my hotel. There are the usual exchanges between the driver and me (a series of firm "No thanks you's," tiredly delivered, with neither irritation nor fervor). It has been almost a year, but it feels far, far longer. If there is any measure of life after death Nigel is watching. Henshaw too believe it or not. He has keeled over on a golf course in Boca Raton, so I am told, and was buried right there, near his new home. (I have not written or sent flowers. To whom would I send them, after all? To Grace, newly divorced? To his chippy, whom I once asked to make me a Xerox copy?) It would be a profound disappointment to me if there were an afterlife, even more so if there were one in which the sorry pursuits of one bald man were worth taking time out from the music of harps and the pleasures offered by seventy virgins.

As I jostle about on the taxi seat, overtired, overwrought, I can see the meeting of those two who never met in corporeal life quite clearly. They will, soon enough, discover their common acquaintance. Each will have something to say.

"He's right down there," Henshaw will say, pointing at this dented car through the clouds. "Meeting that desperate little human need we all once had."

"No, no," Nigel will reply, coming to my defense. "He went there for that reason, but the irony is that once he had lanced the pent-up zeal, he found himself at a loss. It was all so much easier than he had imagined, don't you see – this one, that one, any one – and it all came to seem quite silly, if you want to know the truth of it. Anyone for a song means the whole thing loses its allure. His desires turned soft, not to put too fine a point on it, and he began seeking something more elusive. He's not a satyr, that round little Buber down there. He's a romantic, a hopeless romantic."

Well, I hope that's what he says, and I really don't care much what Henshaw might think to say in reply. Thinking that Nigel might come to my defense allows me to smile through the smudgy window at the weltering other world outside.

I sit on the sticky seat and watch the buildings flash by. It is hot, moist, and smelly; there is a recklessness to it, a gaudiness to it, to the bare-chested laborers at the side of the road, to the people wedged into smoking samlors, to the soiled storefronts, sooty shutters, unkempt overpasses. We pass the staggering temples with their *stupas* and *chedis*, their

170

rows of saffron monks, pass the elaborate ceramic roofs, the beautiful girls, the beautiful boys, and there is some strange disconnected junction in it all, how it all fits together. Lurid things and spiced foods and bright lights and turgid rivers merge in the heat and the night. The air that seeps into the car swirls with spice and sweat.

I had thought I would have moments of doubt, have dreaded their advent, but there are none now. I have an address, the one to which my checks have been sent for over a year, and of course there is the Star of Love Bar. Pla and others will know exactly where to find her. I know what I will say when I see her. I know what I will do. There will be no floundering, not this time. I do not care, believe it or not, what I may find. It will change nothing for me even if I show up at the Star of Love Bar and find her, the woman for whom I have crossed the world, on her knees once again.

Such things matter not at all.

At the hotel I unpack my suitcase, shower, try to sleep, but it is not possible, and so I dress and take an elevator to the lobby. I wander past the gift shops, a restaurant, a group of men, Germans by the sound of it, talking loudly and laughing in sudden, graphic bursts. With them are several Asian girls who stand quietly, hold the men's hands, appear to be interested in what is being said even as they say nothing themselves. They are dressed in similar strappy dresses, one of them in tight jeans, and I wonder how it must feel for girls so small and demure to lie under such large men, men with reddish hair and stomachs bulging and perspiration coating their faces. I could not stand in a hotel lobby pawing a prostitute and making raucous jokes. In the end I have learned that I cannot be one person in one place and another simply because I am elsewhere.

The restaurant is almost deserted except for a table in the corner where a man and a woman appear to be deep in some intimate discussion. I take a seat and then a family enters, an Arab family by the look of it, the men in floppy white pajamas and the women covered from head to foot in black. How does that work, I mutter into the menu, burkha-clad primitives in this museum of the carnal? I examine the menu, order. When the food arrives I find that I cannot eat more than a few mouthfuls. I really am now very tired indeed.

I feel safe, not lonely at all. The peace of it, the freedom and the license of it, could be addictive.

∽

It is dawn and the sky assumes an unearthly gold cast. Perhaps it is the unclean air, perhaps the sun reflecting off the brown waters of the river, perhaps it is the yellow streaks rising from the golden spires and temple mounds that lace the city, that turns the air so gold. Already the tempo is fast, jittery, pungent. There are people everywhere.

"You come with me," a tout says, taking hold of my arm as I leave the hotel.

I smile, take it back, shake my head. The optimism has not abated. Things will be okay. I approach the taxi rank and when the drivers see me they come at me in a phalanx, offering better deals, daylong service, whatever it is I care to have. One of them, an older man, has something about him that appeals to me and I walk in his direction. He sweeps at me and shepherds me to his car, gesturing, opening the door, making an elaborate show of dusting off the seat.

"Where to?" he asks.

I hand him Nok's address and he studies it, frowns.

"Wait please," he says and steps from the car.

For the first time I feel an edge of doubt, a worry, and I watch the driver carefully as he consults with the others. There are hand gestures, much pointing, and I am reassured.

"Who live here?" he asks when he returns to the car.

"A friend," I say.

"Not so nice place," he says. "Foreigners don't go there. But I can take you if you wish."

"Thank you," I say and settle back into the seat.

We set off through the city, through the clogged streets and the milling crowds. On the sidewalk I see women setting up food stands with sizzling woks and heaps of

172

vegetables, vendors laying out tee shirts and necklaces, souvenirs, plaster Buddhas, great dried insects pinned to velvet boards. Whiffs of incense reach into the car, tinge the fumes and the smoke with a fine, tickling edge. I am excited, keen, fully awake. Today, perhaps, things will change course, begin again. Whatever it is that lies ahead, however ill-advised, precipitate, or foolish, I will go at it with the same vigor and energy I have given to other, less worthy causes.

"You visit friend?" the driver asks, as if seeking confirmation that this expedition is valid, has purpose.

I look into the rearview mirror and see his eyes, slightly bloodshot, his unkempt gray eyebrows, a shock of hair across his forehead. From behind he looks younger, all ears and unshaved neck.

"I am going to see the woman I love," I say.

I want to hear myself say this, to feel the words, to sit with the idea as it makes its way into the air.

"A local lady?" the man asks.

He is watching me carefully, curiously.

"Yes," I say. "I am going to marry her."

"Aha," he says, understanding, and then he chuckles. "You brave man."

"Why brave?" I ask, taking the bait, but he says nothing.

We drive on in silence and soon it is clear that we have left behind the modern city with its white buildings and plate glass storefronts. There are no westerners about now, few other taxis. The streets are narrow and the buildings are moldy.

"Are we almost there?" I ask.

The driver does not answer, but gestures instead to the corner ahead and makes his way to the side of the road. He turns off the engine and opens the door.

"I come with you," he says. "Show you."

"Don't worry," I say. "I'll be okay from here. I'll ask for help if I need it."

"This one," he says ignoring me. He walks away from the car, returns and gestures for me to follow.

I stand on the sidewalk, the only westerner in sight, and watch as he enters an alley, beckons for me to follow. It would be a simple matter, I know, for him to double-cross me, for him to rob or molest me and then disappear like a puff of smoke.

"This one, really," he says.

So I am on guard, apprehensive, but what choice is there, after all, now that I have come so far? There are puddles of old water, scraps of newsprint, a sudden coolness in the shade.

"This one," the man says, and he points to a small brick building in need of paint, a single step, a wooden door, lines of rust weeping from the windows.

———

Persuading the embassy (it is, when all is said and done, an embassy) to give Nok a visa to the United States is not a simple matter. They need reassurance, of course, that she will not ever be a liability, that she will comply with the terms of her visa, that she will not disappear into the who-knows-what world of domestic service and, perhaps, prostitution. These things are not unknown. Earnest though I may be, they are certain at the embassy that they know better, that they have seen it all. Beyond the forms, then, there is the scrupulously detailed interview I will have to sit through, alone, in some discomfort. It is no stretch to anticipate what the little foreign service upstart examining me will think of it all, but I am, after all, a citizen, and bringing the woman I intend to marry to my home is something I am entitled to do. I can prove I intend to do just that. I am certainly able to finance it. The ordeal should be limited to an exchange of bank papers and a rubber stamping.

The matter is, of course, somewhat more complex than that, but the obstacles are not insurmountable. How did I meet her, I am asked, and of course the question is a trick one, one that cannot be answered truthfully, but that cannot also—not to put too fine a point on it—be answered untruthfully. I have an obligation not to lie to my government under oath, and even if I did there is a limit to how much artifice poor Nok could carry in her head when it is

174

her turn, as indeed it will be, to answer similar questions seated alone in this forbidding little room of theirs. And, I mean, they're not blind at the embassy. Absent some policy or other, I wouldn't doubt the youngster questioning me has done his tour of duty at the Star of Love Bar himself.

There is a picture of George W. Bush on the wall. He sits with his little elfin grin and watches the proceedings. How did I meet her?

I met her, I say, through a friend, Pla, who is indeed a sex worker, though the name of the establishment at which she works eludes me now. I went up-country to meet her family, stayed with them, in fact, formed a close and cordial friendship with her father, my future father-in-law. A person wouldn't do that, surely he would agree, unless he were deadly serious in his enterprise. And yes, of course I am aware that in this culture the sort of marriage I am contemplating carries with it certain obligations to the intended's family, but the economic divide is so large, don't you know, that I can fulfill such obligations without even feeling it. I mean—again not to put too fine a point on it—look at my bank statement. At my stock portfolio.

I am talking too much, too fluidly. He is watching with a measure of skepticism, but he knows too that he cannot push all this too far. He has a certain amount of discretion, to be sure, but I am also a citizen, and a lawyer aware of my rights, and by all accounts rather more affluent than the average beach boy who gets a similar idea into his mind after falling for one of the locals. In the end, after a rather grueling couple of hours, a wait of several weeks, I will get my permission.

"I think this will be okay," the youngster will have to conclude when he is done, though it is clear that his skepticism will not have abated. "Good luck."

Nok will have been waiting outside and we will hail a samlor, steam off down the street for a celebratory lunch. There has been one obstruction after another, but this, with luck, will be the last. When they call you, I say, remember what we said about how we met, about my trip to your village, about your desire someday to be a nurse. Remember

175

what we agreed we would say about what you have been doing since I left here, how you feel about me, about coming to America, about marriage. Keep these things straight and we should be home free. The samlor driver yells at a friend who pulls up alongside. Nok squeezes my hand, runs her fingers along my leg. "I so happy, Alfie," she says. "You good man. I try be good wife."

So idyllic, so perfect, like a perfect yuppie couple registering at Bloomingdale's in anticipation of their upcoming nuptials at one or another of the city's stylish venues.

"I so happy too," says Rudyard the Kipling, his desires stirred, into the bargain, by the delicate brown fingers running up his thigh. "I don't know why I waited so long. Everything is going to turn out great."

—⊶⊷—

I stagger through the smoke-bound streets, past the little tarts wagging their bodies at me, to the steaming doors of the Star of Love Bar. The yellow fog rubs its back upon the window panes. The yellow smog licks its tongue into the corners of the evening. Nothing has changed, nothing at all. Women in red robes sit on stools that line the entrance and display slits of brown leg. As I approach they begin their suggestive calls. There are walls of sound, waves of people, a crushing overload of this and that. None of the women at the entrance is familiar, but as I step through the door the call is familiar, the welcomes and the hello sirs. These are exactly the same.

I allow myself to be led to the crescent-shaped couches, to be handed a cola, to be smothered in legs and arms, before I come to the point. At the address to which my checks were once sent, Nok is a mystery. There is a girl in her room, two of them in fact, their mattresses lying side by side on the floor, and they have invited me in, wanted me to come in, welcomed the customer fallen unasked for from the sky—but they are not Nok. The dinginess of the place has caught me off-guard too, the state of the paint, peeling, discolored, the single neon strip at the ceiling that gives everything a dank, pasty feel. The room is hot, wet and swampy, claustrophobic. There isn't even a real bathroom, but rather a closet with a stone basin and a cup for ladling water, a commode, a tiny sink against the wall, a single hand towel draped over a pipe. If I had to live there I would paint the walls white, empty the room of its fake mahogany bureau, of all the warping pictures, of the steel bed, make room for the air to move. I would sleep on a mattress and leave room to swing my arms, to walk, to breathe.

They know nothing of Nok, these recent arrivals. The room had belonged to someone else before them. That person is long since gone.

"Nok?" they repeat to each other after me. "Nok?"

There are torrents of conversation, a call to the person who lives next door, but it seems, it has always seemed, as if the collective memories of this place are no more than an inch thick, no more than five minutes deep.

"Nok?" the neighbor says, eyeing me keenly. "Nok?"

So much headshaking, so much animated discussion.

"Nok," I repeat as if this is some sort of mantra, a clue of sorts to one of life's complex mysteries. "I am looking," I say, "for someone called Nok."

Why this triggers the excited, the extensive dialog it does, the irrelevant stream of questions (Where you see her? How you know her? You write her here?), I cannot fathom. I try in broken English to tell them something of the story, but gradually, imperceptibly, I see that they are losing interest. They know what they need to know of it. Why not just pick one of them, their eyes say, and call it a day?

The blank faces have driven me on to the Star of Love Bar where once again Nok's name draws a blank, as does that of Pla. I find myself aping the fish mouth once again, drawing my jowly lips into her little pouty underbite. Surely if anyone here knew her this display would be sufficiently distinctive. Pla's name now follows Nok's into their sentences, their headshakings, the earnest withdrawal of hands from my crotch as the business at hand is debated.

"You know her from here?" the bartender, an older gent, worldly wise, all business says. "Why not, sir, take another girl. Many girls here. Girls come and go. I don't know where that one is."

("Relax mate," I hear an Australian say to his companion being serviced beside him at the bar. "You look like you're taking a calculus final.")

Personnel records, I want to suggest, this laughable fool fresh out of Boston. Don't you keep a W-2 form somewhere, a forwarding address, a reference source? The older gent—my age perhaps but it is hard to tell with these people—has an inspiration, remembers a secret weapon. He calls into the darkness and a girl comes forward. This one is braiding her hair, has large round eyes and a face of painted innocence. The others, those about me, descend into laughter and our gathering takes on the ambience of a slumber party rather than a bordello. Two of the girls get up and start to dance with each other in the aisle.

The child, and she is a child, sits beside me.

"This one, sir, has just arrived," the bartender tells me. "Yesterday."

She puts her hand on my thigh, of course. It seems to be so standard on this street that it must be contained in a procedures manual. She begins to do the stroke.

"How old is this girl?" I ask, looking carefully at her face.

"Fifteen," the man says. "She new."

"Pipteen," the girl says, seriously, softly.

The bartender walks out from behind the bar, joins our little group.

"She baby," he says. "Men like. You like?"

"Now see here," thunders Mother Theresa. "This girl is too young to be working at this job. Too young," I repeat, pointing at her face, gesturing up and down at her tiny little frame.

Oh, I am the subject of such merriment, such entertainment. One of the girls grabs the newcomer's robe and pulls it open, cups one of her breasts, tilts it in my direction. Another, cottoning on to the humor of it, slides a hand between her thighs, probes lewdly with her finger. The slumber party gathers momentum.

(I do not need a lecture on virtue. I deliver them myself, thank you very much.)

"Not baby," the girl insists. *"Pipteen."*

I am on the verge of tears. Is this all it reduces to? Is this it, this the sum total of the months of imaginings, countless facile little thoughts as I wobbled around my garden, panted along the bike path, munched on watercress and sticks of celery? Is this where it ends, Buber's career, his thoughts, his life itself?

But human beings are, I suppose, human beings, and the bartender senses that something has gone awry. Something in it draws out the decency in him. A harsh word or two and the festivities cease, the girls withdraw. He pours me a beer of his own accord and one for himself, returns and seats himself beside me.

"Tell me everything you can," he says. "People come and go a lot around here, but I will try and help."

Where to start is not difficult given where we are, and when I am done he becomes thoughtful, begins questioning the girls who surround us, who have been listening with care, those more facile in English filling in for the others what they have missed. Help comes in the form of a slim girl in her mid-twenties, I would guess, who, if I can trace the outlines of my visit to Nok's village, will fill in the details, translate, guide me right back to that house on stilts.

It is an assignment that perplexes her. I will have several times to explain, in words and gestures, that sexual services are not required of her as part of her mission. In the end she will settle down into her role of translator, intermediary, guide, silent companion.

She is, I would have to say, something of a trooper.

Hester Prynne Buber, a gigantic 'W' etched in red on his chest (for whoremonger, don't you know), sits once again with his legs dangling off the back of a tumbrel on his way to a rendezvous even more futile, even more pathetic, than the last. The countryside ambles by, the ox drawing us walks with deliberation, the child at my side takes it all in with an impressive nonchalance. There is dust on my clothes, dust in my hair, dust in the lining of my lungs. A rice farmer or two looks up at this strange vision, at this absurd little Chautauqua, turns his attention back to the muck at his feet.

Oh great puritanical God: Let them be wrong about this. Let her be there.

My father-in-law, it seems, is off in the field. I have clambered up the rickety stairs and onto the platform above the trees, and there are the bed mats stacked against the walls, the pots, the wicker chair, the stained floor. There is the spot I slept in, the place I was ill, the corner—so Nok has told me—she herself had occupied as a girl. Up here on the platform, I suddenly notice, it is cooler than it is just ten feet below. There are brushes of wind, a clarity of air, a sense of space. The fields below are coated with plantings of the most vivid green. Clumps of palm trees provide a rich and exotic texture. Water buffalo move slowly down watery furrows.

A child in the near distance sees me, a small, dusty girl with improbably shining hair, and I wave. What a spectacle it must be, indeed, lost foreigner up on stilts where the likes of him were never meant to be. She stands for a moment fixed to the spot and then, instead of waving back, begins to run and I hear her thin voice, a series of excited shouts.

My Star of Love guide, standing beside me, mutters.

"What was that?" I ask.

"She frightened," she says, and laughs. "Maybe first time American come to this place."

"No," I remind her. "I have been here."

She nods, but does not, still and after I have with her help brought us this far, completely believe me.

"You were here? In this house?"

"Yes," I say, exasperated. "That's how I knew how to find it."

Well, that's not strictly true. Picking our way across the landscape, my guide and I, it has all begun to look the same, has seemed quite ludicrous. Our reaching here at all has been a matter of the greatest serendipity. We have made so many mistakes, seen so many dead-end lanes, places that looked familiar and then turned out to be quite different than I had expected, that it is almost a miracle that we are here at all. I could not give up. I could not. And then something did look familiar, and continued to do so, and we have now, in the end, reached Nok's house.

"These people very poor," she says. "Many farmers poor, but these people have nothing."

She looks about her and a measure of distaste shows on her face.

"House dirty," she adds. "This one your girlfriend family house?"

"Yes," I say and then, I can't help myself it seems, I add: "It's not so bad."

The little girl below reappears in the distance, followed now by several adults. My guide and I climb carefully down the ladder and begin to walk towards them. There is mud about and I step into a puddle of sorts. The mud oozes over the top of my loafers, sinks into my socks. I try to rub my shoe against some grass as I walk, reach the little reception party like someone with a club foot.

"Good morning," I say full of cheer.

The mad German baron, descended from his castle laboratory to discuss the progress of his experiments with the townsfolk, each of whom would have been carrying a pitchfork, may have received a less curious reception.

———⚬⚬⚬———

This is all, of course, a cascade of desperate acts. After I left the Star of Love Bar I returned to my hotel, suddenly immeasurably tired, and fell asleep in my clothes on the hotel bed. When I awoke I could not tell whether it was seven in the evening or seven in the morning, whether I had slept for two hours or for fourteen. I looked out the window and saw the lights of the city, that it was night, but even so I felt upside down, as if it was a new day and not the end of an old. The night still stretched ahead ominously.

I showered, dressed, walked down the stairs to the lobby. I am not a drinker, not really. I nurse a brandy most evenings, more an aid to contemplation than anything else, but in truth I do not care for the taste of most spirits. I seat myself in the lounge and order a gin, and then another, and then things begin to acquire a roseate tinge, to lose their desolation, not to seem so bad. My chair faces the entrance to the hotel massage parlor, an international standards brothel just a hundred feet away. I could stagger in, be greeted with charm, be poked and pulled at, and yet despite a lifetime of yearning there is of it now not even a distant memory.

I stay and drink, one gin after another until I can barely order, though even so the polite young man serving me does not show any judgment or disapproval. I slur my words, lean crookedly into the chair, watch with a wonky, disconnected kind of curiosity as people come and go. So this is how it feels, I think, to detach, to allow things simply to flow about you without concern, to be an island, insensate, in the stream.

"May I show you to your room?" the young man asks.

A glass has tumbled off the arm of the chair, lies shattered on the marble floor. He mops it up, still with the same unflinching discretion.

I look up into his face, a smiling, young, handsome face.

"It's that obvious," I mutter and he, not understanding, helps me to my feet and guides me to the elevator.

When I wake I am wearing only my underwear, see that my clothes have been folded and hang over the back of a chair. My canvas pouch and money belt are lying side by side on the bedside table, and when I check them I see that nothing has been touched. I have, of course, a pounding headache, but I haul myself from the bed and step into the shower, let the water drum on me as if the needles themselves could get under my skin and scour away all that is jaundiced and impure.

I have been drunk in a hotel at the end of the planet, have been helped to my bed, and have been undressed and left to sleep by a stranger. Oh dear, oh dear.

This, then, is how I start out on my mission to find Nok in the countryside.

What shall I do now? What shall I do?
I shall rush out as I am, and walk the street.

No, humble peasants, I have not come here to sever your heads and perform experiments on you. I am, remember now, the man who came here with Nok just under a year ago, the one who took you all, this household and the next, the whole village it seemed at the time, to a restaurant of sorts a short tractor-pull away.

Glimmers of recognition, shouts of recognition, the farmer with large gaps in his mouth recognizes the man to whom he sold his daughter.

"Short time, only," he says, and for a moment I am puzzled at his meaning, but then it descends on me with a crash: He thinks I have come for my money back, honest to God. He thinks I have come to get back from him my five hundred dollars.

"No, no, no, no," I say, raising my hands quickly, disarmingly, laughing. "Please tell him," I say to my guide, "that I have not come to complain. That I don't want anything from him."

She's not quite sure, it is obvious, what this is all about, but she does the best she can; and from what I can see—and there are a lot more words exchanged here than the relatively simple idea I have wished to convey—the old man's tone softens.

"He asks," she says finally, and with a simplicity that would be amusing if it were not all so, well, absurd, "why you come here?"

It is a businesslike question, asked in a businesslike manner. We are not going to share once again, he and I, this is clear, the *bonhomie* of relatedness, or if we are it is equally clear that more money is going to have to change hands.

"I'm looking for Nok," I say, and this is not news to him because, while I can decipher none of what has passed between him and my interlocutor, this is a word I have recognized. Nok has already been, and several times, mentioned.

"Nok not here," my Star of Love Bar guide says without revisiting the old man. "Nok gone."

This much I have already ascertained on my own.

"Where is she?" I ask, and I try to keep my voice calm, to betray nothing.

Another dialog ensues and through some of it I allow my attention to wander, conclude that in the end this is all part of another negotiation, that when all is said and done it will reduce to a request for money, money which, of course, I will be only too glad to part with. It goes without saying, legend has it, that acquiring a wife from these parts means acquiring the penury of her family. Good and well.

But then, of course, there creeps into the discussion a tone I do not welcome, something new, hands flicking away, up into the distance, and then words I do recognize, so God help me, "London" and "UK" among them, and I am certain this is my imagination, a host of hidden fears peeping out of nowhere to taunt me except that he says it again: "London." And in that instant the countryside changes, its promise evaporates, the squalor and the poverty and the mud, the filthy buffalo and the hardscrabble people become as clear as silhouettes. The future shifts in a precipitous and alarming way.

I interrupt.

"What did he say about London?" I ask. "What has London to do with this?"

—◦◦◦◦—

I will dither no further. She has learned a trade, I piece together bit by bit from the girl, as she translates one after another the long, impatient, petulant, impenetrable

184

statements of the father. Later, sitting on a plastic stool in the Star of Love Bar, I learn the rest from the bartender who has done his own homework in my absence. She has remained in the city but not returned to the bar or to the business plied there. She has taken my money, or so it appears, and learned to be a clerk in an office, has found a job, reported each day in a trim blue uniform to stack paper for the copy machine and make the coffee, has found a room, bought a few things, collected a paycheck, been diligent, been prompt.

She has caught the eye of a young Englishman, "England man," the bartender calls him, sent out to work in this office, a young manager of sorts out for foreign adventure. He has asked her out on a date as normal people do, timorously I would have to imagine. In due course, he makes his own way out to this remote and horrible village, meets the father, pays the bounty. In the last couple of months he has been posted back to England and has taken his new wife with him, his lovely, innocent, clean, lithe, wholesome new wife.

I am pushed back on my heels, back on my heels again and again as this is unfolded for me, as the story is unpeeled and placed before me in all its layers. The mouths telling it, the faces telling it, tell it as if it is just information, just a story to be told, just facts to be passed along to the fat and sweating man who sits there pumping them for details even as each of them is a white pin stuck into his eyes. More please, and more please, and more please.

She is gone, and that is that, and whatever is left is whatever is left.

———

Well, not so fast. I leave with my Star of Love guide on the back of the same ox wagon—we are gouged for the return trip, but what is the alternative? To wait indefinitely in the field until another option presents itself?—and jostled slowly, in the rhythm of the countryside, back to a depot where we are to catch a bus to the same rickety half-way hotel where Nok and I first spent a night in each other's arms. As the cart rattles over the pitted lane I stew, am in ferment over my lost Nok, over the chance for happiness that my foolishness, my bashfulness, my very Buberness, has forfeited.

"Wait," I say to the girl and she says nothing, allows the cart to continue its grind.

"No," I say. "Stop this cart."

She stares at me, a look of pity now crossing her face.

"Girl gone," she says. "Nok gone with England man."

"I need to talk to her father again," I say. "I want to talk to Nok's father," I repeat, slowly, deliberately, with all the clarity and calm I can muster. "I must talk to him."

Now she does instruct the driver to stop and he does it ponderously, pulls on a yoke, dithers as the ambling continues. He calls out to the animal, clucks and whistles until it comes to a stop, turns expectantly in my direction.

"Tell him to take us back," I say.

My guide explains what it is I have said and the man fails to respond, remains as silent and as obdurate as his ox. When he does talk it is a few mumbled words only. Without understanding any of them, his attitude is no secret.

"I will pay," I say. "Of course I will pay."

We are an hour or so gone and my exact wishes cannot be, it appears, communicated or understood without a lengthy exchange. A lengthy exchange there is, filled with glances at me, at this ridiculous Bubonic plague of a foreigner, with expressions changing from disdain to disbelief to pity. I listen to the furious exchange, and without even bothering to ask what it means I nod as I watch the rubbing together of the driver's thumb and forefinger, the warning to this crazy white ghost that a price has been negotiated, is firm, is set in stone, and that beyond it everything else will cost dearly. Finally the man turns back to his animal, instructs us off the cart as he negotiates its turn, begins to move back in the direction from which we have just come, leaving us to trot after him and to clamber aboard.

I will spare you the scene at our return, the incredulity, the scorn, the look on her father's face as his vigorously shaking head begins to slow in time to the notes peeling

186

away from my wallet, as his expression softens as one note after another quiets his fury and transforms our interaction to one of business: a postcard with an address printed on it in exchange for the sheaf that has been slowly built, one by one, from the notes that slide from my wallet. All eyes are on it, on the wallet, not a one on my face, and I welcome the privacy this affords me. In London, I imagine, there are not many girls who resemble Nok. As she moves down the street men must turn and look at her, admire the deftness of her movements, how her legs wind about each other as she moves, like licks of flame climbing a pole. I am not certain, to be perfectly honest about it, to complete this Log entry with honesty, as I clutch the postcard in my hand — on one side is a picture of the Tower of London, on the other a message in a language I do not read, but also an address, an address — what exactly I plan to do with this information I have just bought from Nok's faithless father.

─── ⬠ ───

In the dusty hotel at which my guide and I finally arrive, late at night, we are shown to our shared room, and all along I am entertaining the absurd notion of flying off to London, of posting myself outside the house whose address I have been given, determining for myself, finding out for myself, whether she is happy, whether it is permanent, whether there is any chance she might want, might consider, coming back to me.

I stretch out on the bed, kick off my shoes, listen as the girl goes into the bathroom and runs the water, drinks, rattles around with her bottles and brushes. She returns to the room naked except for a towel, and it makes no difference, does not matter. I have no interest in it, in her.

"I massage," she says, and I would decline except there is something gentle in her tone, something that is not suggestive, that is not lewd.

I say nothing and she removes my trousers, my shirt, begins to push about at my flesh, to flex and bend the muscles in the calf, the muscles in my thigh, to press into my fingers and my arms. It occurs to me that this is her act of kindness, that she understands the bereavement in the day, that she is showing a measure of compassion. As she kneads away it occurs to me that whatever it is I do cannot matter that much, really, that the flesh and the fat and the fluid of it are quite transient, unimportant; that to follow through on one's urges is quite mundane really, as mundane as the pulling and the pushing, this muscle, that, this organ that, this pleasure that. I am alone on a bed in the middle of nowhere, in the last quadrant of my life, without point of reference, without censor, without guardian. Nok is somewhere, not gone yet, merely a distance to cover. All may not be lost. Reason must prevail, reason and history and the sheer depth of it, must prevail.

In the morning we catch the train back to the city, traipse along the dusty streets to my hotel, and there my guide leaves me.

"Good luck," she says. "I want you to have good luck."

"Thank you," I say, and then of course, acting in the only way I know how, I hand her a sheaf of bills larger I would bet than any she has seen. She thanks me delicately, and then I wait on the hotel step as the doorman hails her a taxi and she slips into the backseat, a trim, fresh, uneducated girl. As she closes the door she is transformed, lighter, gives her instruction to the driver with all cheer, settles back into the seat.

I am nauseated by the aromas, irritated by the touts, have little stomach for the monks in their saffron robes, the roar of the traffic, the constant thump of music and machinery.

———

There is one final thing I should mention about my portfolio. I have kept, for reasons so opaque I could not begin to unravel them, some money in a numbered account in Switzerland. You will find the number and the codes you will need taped to the underside of my desk drawer. You should know, of course, that this is illegal. American citizens may not keep caches of undeclared money to earn interest in foreign banks. My doing it anyway has to do with some weakness in me, an unremitting fear that the roof may, without a clear precursor, fall in. I do not want again to be a refugee carting his bedroll on a wagon.

———⁂———

I landed at Heathrow airport late in the afternoon and then, still dazed from the trip, the time change, the strange food, unshaven too I would have to add, I stored my possessions at left luggage and took a black taxi, one of those rattling antique bathtubs, from the airport rank to the address I had been husbanding in my pocket. It was dark when I got there, raining lightly. The row house outside which I stood looked modest but well-kept. The lights were on. I went to the front door, rang the bell, waited. There were footsteps, the handle rattled, and then she opened the door.

It was a small English room, one of those rooms where the furniture, arranged around the wall, is nevertheless so close together that one wonders how the occupants' feet don't touch in the middle. The lights were on, a lamp was on, there was a carpet on the floor. I could smell cooking. For a long moment, for a very long moment, she and I stood in place, looked into each other's faces, absorbed the shocking sight.

"What you doing here?" she asked at last, her voice hushed, conspiratorial, urgent. "Why you come here, this place?"

"For you," I said. "I have come for you."

"No," she protested, and now her voice rose, became audible, harder. "No, no. I here now. Have husband now."

"You're not married," I said. "Your father told me you were not married."

Now her jaw drops, her mouth literally falls open, her arms — which had been in front of her shushing me out, sweeping, pushing without actually touching me — drop to her sides.

"You saw my father?"

189

"Yes," I say. "I went to your village and I saw him."

She stands in place, awestruck, silent, and then from within, from another room I hear a boy's voice, a callow English voice: "Nok?" it says.

"My husband," she says, and now her tone is on the edge of hysteria and there are, who could not see it coming, tears in her eyes. "My husband," she repeats so urgently, so plaintively, that even I am moved.

"Who is it?" he asks.

"Come outside with me," I whisper. "Just for a moment. Just a few steps, down onto the sidewalk. Just for a moment."

"No," she says, except that now she says it loudly, my Nok, loudly enough that the boy in the other room will hear, deliberately so that the boy in the other room will hear, a betrayal, a sea change, the first step down the rungs of this thing, a summons. "No," she repeats. "I not talk with you. You go."

Oh my Nok.

"You go," she repeats.

"Not before I talk to you," I say.

I am a creature out of late night television, arrested in his vest by state policemen cruising run-down neighborhoods in garish cars.

"I must," I say. "I love you. I do. I still do."

"What the devil is this?" the boy, who now appears in the frame left by the door, the lamps, the dead carpet, the orange light, asks.

He is wearing ugly English clothes, gray pants, laced shoes, a white tee shirt. His blond hair, cropped, is untidy and on his large biceps there are tattoos, one of a shapely woman with a dragon wrapped around one leg, another of a female face with a finger at the lip.

"Who are you, mate?" he asks. "What are you doing here?"

His breath smells faintly of beer and of tobacco. Oh Nok. Oh Nok. He is so young, so brawny. His accent reveals that he drives a bus, or carries bricks, or empties cans.

"My name is Alfred Buber," I say. "I am a lawyer from America. I have known your wife for a long time."

"Sounds to me like you're bothering her," is all he says and turning to Nok he adds, "Do you know him? Do you?"

Nok looks at me and in her face now there is something I recognize, something I wish I had not seen. In her face is desperation.

"I know," she says. "A long time ago I know. A little."

"Well, what do you want?' he demands. "This is England. We're here now. Whatever happened before, happened. Get it mate?"

"Please," I say, and we are seconds away now, I must add if the reading of this is too tedious, too tortured, the begging, the ridiculousness of it too much even after all that I have already revealed, seconds away from the end of it all. "I need to talk to this woman. Please."

"I don't know what you're smoking," the boy says and Nok, standing behind him, taking shelter behind him, continues to hold my eye, fear in her face, fear and distaste and shock. A new roundness, a flatness, has come quickly to her lovely face. "But you'd better get a move on."

"Nok," I plead, but I can't do this, can I, participate in this. Concentrate on the stocks, then, the bank accounts, the money and the land, the patios and the sweeping lawn, the man who will bring a crate of flightless birds in the Spring to strut about on the grass. There is a hand now on my shoulder, a firm English brutish hand on my shoulder, pale skin, freckles, ginger hairs, there is a face close to mine, angry eyes. I am told I don't get it, but I do, I do. I get that this is the last moment, the last chance, I cannot relent, and then I make a mistake. I push back as hard as I can, and he falters for just a moment, and then there is a blur of pushing and flailing—and I may make further gestures that are inappropriate—and then I am hit in the jaw and more than once, and then there is a man in a blue uniform standing over me, handcuffs on my wrists, statements being taken.

Am I done? Am I quite done? Do I care at all? The answer would be no, the answer is no, except for one thing, one small thing, and that is that when they have taken me in the backseat of one of those screeching English cars with its blue light and its coughing radio to a station house somewhere and I have filled out forms, submitted to whatever it is I am supposed to submit to, a burning in my eye, blood in my mouth, a tooth gone, there is the question of bail, the question of the circumstances under which I am to be released. And I see that my wallet—in the tumult—my passport, are gone, that I have nothing that proves I am who I say I am other than a housebreaker, an intruder, an American intent on molesting a young woman, and that means days and days in this cold and ugly place until someone from the embassy can come and straighten things out. He will contact Henshaw & Potter, I will assume, he will lower the curtain on an act whose end is overdue.

There is another possibility, of course, as I lie there on a bench, my head pounding, my mouth ablaze, my heart so heavy it scarcely seems my chest can contain it.

"Well, we'll have to keep you," I hear, "until we can clear some of this up," but this I cannot withstand. I cannot survive that.

"Is there anyone who can vouch for you?" is the question. "Anyone at all?"

There is an answer to that, of course. There is an answer and by now it is clear what the choice is, this here or that there, no choice at all, no choice at all even though within two hours I will hear the most difficult sentence I have ever had to hear:

"Oh Alfred. I thought you were doing so well."

But I will reveal this, and it surprises even me. The shame of it has healed me. The shame beyond shame has brought an end to the shame even as the thought of it, sitting there at a traffic light in the London traffic, in the searing white heat of a London taxi, even as the thought of it has torn away the entire scaffolding of my life. The taxi is hot, so boiling in fact that the plastic clothes I wear burn into my flesh and leave their mark, so white hot that I am still blinded by the thought of it with my bewildered mother beside me as we make our halting way from the jail to the shabby little flat in Golders Green. And even as the thought of it chills me, burns me, the shame has sunk in and cleansed me of further shame. There is silence, there are furtive, doleful glances, and though several weeks have now passed, it is as vivid as if I were still there now and yet I feel nothing but heat. Nothing but heat.

What has happened both matters and it matters not a whit. I cannot explain it beyond that.

CHAPTER EIGHT

M̲rs. Savage has gone for the day, has made it clear indeed that her days here are numbered. I am not sure I have the full measure of her antagonism but she complains about the distance she must drive, about clearing away cigar ash and the occasional bottle of alcohol, about the nature of the food I ask her to prepare. Soon, within days, I will let her go.

It is very dark here tonight, the whole house in darkness and no moon outside. I sit at my table by the large bay window and from outside I must resemble a gnome, dwarfed as I am by these massive curtains and hunched over this machine tap tapping away. I set out to be honest, to be complete, but a leopard cannot change his spots, can he, and so when you find this tucked away amongst my papers, if you care to find this, you will make of it what you will. I had the choice, as I have already said, simply to burn everything, but I did not. I may have you all wrong, of course. It is likely, quite likely, that I do. I have lost, you see, all faith in my own judgment. Perhaps these notebooks are the best evidence of that. Present them to the judge, then, if ever I am to be judged. I still have a court date, theoretically, at a magistrate's court outside of London. Charges, I understand, have been pressed. I will not be there to answer them. It may all be, in the end, a puzzle. But I will take my chances on you. I set hereby the record straight or I set it askew. It is all the same to me. The train is in motion regardless, or irregardless as my new countrymen insist on saying.

In the paper, the little tabloid freely available on the streets of my mother's London suburb, *The Golders Green Graphic* I believe it is called, my turbulent evening is laid out in all its splendor. I suppose it is news in its own way. There is a picture of me, small and blurry, although perhaps only to me is it blurry. I do not know when it was taken but it does not flatter. There is a description of the events with which, I suppose, from an objective distance, I would not take issue. My mother made a point of leaving the paper on the table in her little sitting room without comment. I will be gone soon enough, soon enough, but news of this will precede me. How could it not? The ripples of it will make their way inexorably across the ocean and I will see signs of them on peoples' faces, in the streetlights, I will see signs of them in the bank and in the park, polluting the air, seeping into everything. It is already on the internet, I have no doubt of it. Just type in "Buber" and there you will see me as in those late night cable shows of celebrities under arrest, hair flying, wild-eyed, groggy lipped, there shall I be. I could do it myself, this research, if I knew how to work the damned machine (and I have tried, trust me, am told each time I press some button or other that I have performed an "illegal" operation. Even the machine knows, it seems.).

You made it clear when you first rang the bell on my door that you were uncertain, of two minds, as to whether you wanted to have a relationship with me, and what kind of relationship it could be. I will not trouble you further, sweet Alice, but what an irony that I should leave behind, in the end, a Eurasian daughter, if you will pardon the term, a Rosalind all my own. Be wary though Alice, if you are not already, of men. We are not to be trusted. We are misled by features only, by topography (of course you know this) of no lasting import and yet we seem, even the brightest and the most erudite of us, to be untouched by this funda-mental knowledge. Mock the men who nurse delusions that they are, at last and singularly, different. They are not. *They are not.*

I have a final secret and it is the unremitting pain in my chest and arm, something I have been told requires rather urgent intervention. The doctors wish to implant several tubes of wire mesh that they say will hold my arteries open, though to what end they do not say. More scaffolding, some bought time, and all for what? I prefer to let nature take its course. They also say that the pains may be nothing. They may be nothing but I hope they are something, and while I wait, puff at my cigar, sip at my brandy, I picture the blood vessels closing in on themselves and scarring over, covering the insult, the harsh thoughts, with vagueness. Soon I will reach a point where memories are so indistinct that I will think back with neither sadness nor pleasure. Here in my sanctuary, at least, I have reclaimed for a while the satisfactions of the evening: solitude, quiet, anonymity. With luck I will disappear, evaporate, cease to exist. I am a man without belief, you see, simply that. My predicament is as meaningful as a slab of meat on a butcher's counter. Dust, that is what I seek to become. An illusion.

So then Nok will not cruise through my mausoleum, mouth either open in awe or firmly closed in a state of something else. Watching her in her own city, me standing back as she approaches a vendor's stall on the side of the street, I see how small she is even among the things that are meant to surround her. The vendor huffs as she makes her request, serves someone who elbows her aside, finally hands her whatever it is she has requested as if it has all been some great imposition. She takes it, walks back to me, her simple errand done. She is so easily brushed aside, so easily overlooked such a wisp of a human being she is, so spent when I have had my way with her and she lies, curled, under the sheet.

But she is someone's *daughter*, when all is said and done, she is someone's daughter and I have wronged her. Can there be any doubt of that, except that in the process I have done her no more harm than I have done myself.

I have put all this down here for one reason, really, and that is because I see now that there exists something I would never have dreamed possible when I was younger, imperfect though things were even then, and that is a failed life. I have lived a failed life. I am not sure how this comes to be. Maybe I am fatally flawed in some manner. Maybe it is something else. A business that is forever losing money must eventually be closed, deemed a failure. A racehorse that cannot race, put down. And I? I am mired in failure though I do have this to show for having existed, and only this: A daughter I did not know I had, lovely and elegant and fair-minded, or so I imagine. I pass to her a measure of well-being and a measure of advice, to the extent that there is advice tucked somewhere in this long Testament of mine.

If there is penance to be made for anything it may rest in the exposure of my frailty, and in my invitation to you to look deep into the breach and to see and make of it what you will. I regret everything and I regret nothing. I am a man, simply that, and either you will understand or you will not. A life has weight by virtue of it having been lived.

Or at least that is what I must believe.